— Lovelines

ALL THE RIGHT MOVES

LINDA HOLLAN

PAN MACMILLAN

Chapter 1

I had a good life right up until the seventeenth of May this year ... No, a 'good life' is putting it too mildly, I had a great life! So what happened? I'll tell you what happened, my best friend starting going out with Warren Fitzpatrick. Now I'm not the sort of person who can't handle her best friend having other interests. I'm cool about that, and as far as I'm concerned, Melissa's time is her own — I just don't want her wasting it with Warren. You couldn't be more reasonable than that, now could you? But then again, what would you know? You've never met Warren Fitzpatrick.

I suppose if we're ever going to get to the bottom of this mess I'd better fill you in a bit. I'd better tell you the whole story about Warren, and about me and Melissa. Putting it like that makes it sound as though Warren's got some right to be in my life, so on second thoughts I'll tell you about me and Melissa and then, when I've got no choice left, I'll get to the business about Warren. Melissa and I have been best friends for the whole of our lives — literally all our lives. You know how you always seem to end up absolutely detesting the children of your parents' friends? Yeah? Well, Melissa and I are the exception to that rule. Mum and Melissa's mum were friends before we were even born, so Melissa and I have known each other right from the word go. We weren't so cute that we went to the same kindergarten or even the same primary school or anything like that, but we've hung out on the weekends ever since I can remember.

I don't want to bore you to tears, so I won't go into graphic detail about every little thing we ever did together. All I'm going to tell you is that we had the most excellent time doing all the usual stuff little kids do — played in the backyard, put on imaginary plays, did dress-ups, dismembered flies, and tortured the various pets our families had collected. Of course we'd grown out of all of that by the time we went to secondary school together. We were lucky, really, starting at the same school. I used to feel sorry for all the kids who had to walk into the place not knowing anyone at all while I had Melissa and Melissa had me. That sort of stuff doesn't last long though and after a few months everyone was pretty well mixed in together. Melissa and I still stayed best friends, but we did have other friends as well. Talking about all of this feels a bit like looking at old home videos — kind of depressing.

'Claire.' Melissa peered at me from over the top of the book she was reading. 'Stop grunting and sighing, will you? You're putting me off.'

'I was not "grunting". You're so insulting.'

'You were so.' She looked at me suspiciously. 'What are you up to anyway?'

'Nothing,' I said, folding my arm carefully over my diary.

'Don't you know it's a sign of an unbalanced personality to be obsessively secretive?'

'I'm not being secretive. You've just got an excessively long nose when it comes to other peoples' business.'

'Your business is my business. We're friends, remember?'

'How could I forget?' I bent back over my diary and began to write again.

She looked at her watch. 'Warren should be here soon.'

'Here?'

'Of course here. Where else?'

'But I thought we agreed that we'd spend the morning at my place and then go ice skating in the afternoon?'

'Yeah,' Melissa nodded, 'well we're still doing that, but Warren's coming too.'

I tried to keep my face neutral, but the corner of my mouth twisted out of my grip and made a face at Melissa.

'What's that supposed to mean?' she demanded.

'Nothing,' I said, innocently.

'You just pulled a face.'

'Did I? Maybe I've developed a nervous tic.' I began to wink and twitch as if I couldn't control my face.

'It's because I said Warren's coming, isn't it?'

'I thought it was going to be you and me on our own ...' The words escaped me before I had a chance to stop them.

'Honestly, Claire,' Melissa sighed, 'can't you accept the fact that Warren and I are together?'

See! See what I mean? It makes me want to jump out of my chair and hit Melissa over the head with my diary when she says things like that. Just look at the way things end up every time Warren comes into the story. I'm not like that, I swear I'm not like Melissa makes me out

4

to be. I'm not the sort of girl who's jealous of her best friend's boyfriend, but Melissa seems to think I am. And do you know why she thinks I am? Because she can't understand what I've got against Warren. Every time I try to explain that he's a dead loss, she thinks *I'm* the one with the problem. Sometimes — like over the last few weeks — I just give up and pretend I don't mind. Melissa likes it when I do that. She thinks I'm 'getting used' to her going out with a guy. Aggggh! It makes me want to vomit. Her attitude is so patronising. And I'm not just imagining it. She makes it sound like I've got something wrong with me, when all the time it's him — Warren. Warren, Warren, Warren — he's the one who needs to be disposed of. And I can prove it too.

After all, it wasn't like this when Melissa went out with that guy Ranjan. He came from Sri Lanka — not that that had anything to do with it. The point is, I didn't mind him. He was really sweet. It didn't worry me that Melissa spent every waking minute watching every move he made. Naturally Melissa says that doesn't count. She says Ranjan was just a 'nice boy' and that Warren's a different sort of person altogether. As far as I'm concerned, Warren equals dickhead and that's about all he adds up to. And you can bet your life that about half of the rubbish coming out of Melissa's mouth at the moment is pure Warren. I hate thinking of them talking about me when I'm not around.

Warren's the type who's all good looks on the outside and something unmentionably nasty on the inside. It's surprising how often that happens — the better they look the uglier they are. And Warren sure looks good — grey eyes tilting down just a fraction at the end of his face, soft skin without a pimple in sight, wide mouth, and a smile that tricks you into thinking he's nice. I wasn't fooled for long, mind you. I looked right into his eyes and saw the truth. Warren's a fraud. As hollow as a rotten tree trunk. As much as I hate to say it about another human being, if he died tomorrow the world would be a cleaner place to live in. Call it caring for the environment. Honestly, I wouldn't be so bitter and twisted if Melissa would stop pushing him down my throat. Probably, if I didn't have to see him or talk to him, I could think of Warren as just another one of mother nature's failed projects.

'Here he is.' Melissa leapt up out of her chair and went to the window overlooking the front garden. 'He's ten minutes late.' She looked at her watch for the eightieth time.

'Oh, what a pity,' I said softly, hoping she

6

wouldn't notice.

'I'll just go down and let him in.'

'Don't bother.' I waved her back into her chair. 'Dad's downstairs, he'll do it.'

Melissa cocked her head slightly and waited for the sound of the front door lock. A little smile edged on to her face as the murmur of male voices reached up to us from below.

'I hope you're not going to behave like this all afternoon,' I hissed at her.

'Like what?' She looked at me surprised.

'You look like a dog waiting for its master to arrive. You could try and act a little more casually. Have a bit more dignity.'

'You're off.' She looked annoyed.

'Sorry,' I grumbled.

Melissa didn't answer, just glared at me in a way that made me realise I hadn't really done much to win her over to my point of view. I thought about going into a lengthy apology, but there wasn't enough time for that — Warren walked in the door, smiled at Melissa and winked at me.

'Hi there,' he drawled.

'Hi, sweetie,' chirped Melissa, kissing him on the cheek.

I just groaned and slowly closed my diary.

'So what have you girls been up to?' Warren

7

looked at us indulgently.

'Just — '

'Nothing,' I said, cutting Melissa off. 'What time is it? Shouldn't we be getting out of here if we want to get a good pair of skates?'

'It's a bit early,' Melissa said.

'Let's go anyway,' I said, wanting Warren out of my house.

'Your word is my command.' Warren held open the door and rolled his eyes over me.

I had no choice but to walk out of the room under his gaze, but as soon as I got to the top of the stairs I hurtled down, three steps at a time to put a bit of distance between us. Out on the street I felt better. Somehow Warren didn't feel so close with a bit of fresh air around me. The ice skating rink was only about ten blocks from my place, so we always walked there. This time I went in front and left the two of them to make fools of themselves where I couldn't see them. It was cold and windy outside. I pulled my duffle coat tight and stared at the grey sky reaching down to meet the road. Some council workers had made matters worse by lining my street with foreign trees which poked their bare branches up into the air. They looked cold and I felt cold. At least with a couple of gum trees I would've been able to pretend it was a dreary spring day. But the way things were, there was no doubting it was mid-July.

'Let's run,' Melissa suggested, the end of her nose turning red with cold. 'My feet are freezing.'

'You two go ahead. It doesn't worry me,' I lied.

Warren grabbed Melissa's hand and they pulled away from me, laughing at the enormous white clouds made by their steaming breath.

'See you there.' Warren winked at me for the second time in ten minutes.

I watched them race towards the intersection of Mahoney's Road and then I lost sight of them as my street took them away towards the park. I felt better on my own anyway. It's hard being around people who are happy all the time — hard for me. The happier they were the worse I felt. And when I got low enough, I couldn't help wondering if Melissa might just be a little bit right. Maybe I was just being jealous and unfair . . .

I came to a stop and leant against a damp picket fence. The question was, did I really want to hang around those two for the rest of the afternoon? Sure, they were expecting me to be there, but then again it wasn't as if they really wanted to skate with me. All they'd be doing would be circling around and around the rink, holding hands. I'd be left, bad skater that I was, about three metres behind them, constantly crashing into the edge of the barrier.

That was all right when Melissa and I were mucking around together. It was funny then, but it wouldn't be funny today. It wouldn't be funny with Warren around. I half sat with my back against the fence and wondered what to do. It didn't make sense to go skating if I didn't really want to — and I didn't. In fact, I'd probably be doing everyone a favour if I didn't turn up. I stood up again and stretched the cold out of my aching legs. I wouldn't go home straight away though. The day wasn't all that bad, not once you'd warmed up a bit. Besides, it was nice being outside. I'd keep going, and before anyone could spot me from the rink, I'd cut across the park and take the long way home. Melissa would let me hear about it later of course, but who cared?

I walked on until I could see Melissa waiting for me outside the rink. Warren must've gone inside already. I hovered behind a tree and felt guilty. This wasn't the way to do things. I knew that if I hurried I could disappear without her seeing me, but what sort of person hides from their best friend? Not me. I stepped out from where I was standing and walked purposefully towards the recreation centre. All I needed now was for 'Sweetie' to come out and spot me! My luck held though, and I reached Melissa standing quietly under the eves, before Warren had a chance to put in an appearance.

'You took your time.' She grinned at me. 'I told Warren to go on in. You know how impatient he is.'

'Yeah,' I nodded. 'Sorry to keep you waiting.'

Melissa took a step towards the front door.

'Look, Melissa, would you mind all that much if I changed my mind?' I asked, really casually.

She sighed. 'What is it now?'

'Honestly, it's not that Warren's with us,' I lied. 'I just don't really feel like skating. I might go for a walk and then head back home and read. I guess I didn't realise how cold it was until I got out. What weather to skate in!' I rolled my eyes.

'What do you think winter's for?' Melissa grinned at me. 'Ice skating … Ice … Mean anything to you? Any bells ringing in that woolly head of yours?'

'Yeah I know, I know. Can I helpt it if the Europeans have such barbaric habits? Personally I like Australian sports. And if I'm forced into any of those imported ones, I insist on more clement weather.'

'Clement?'

'Mild,' I explained. 'I looked it up in the dictionary this morning.'

11

'I can just imagine what you're going to be like when you're older.' She made a face. 'You're going to get worse and worse, you know. I've got a great aunt like you. We all just smile and nod when she comes at Christmas time. Look, I'd better go in.' She peered over her shoulder at the front door. 'Warren will be wondering.'

'And we wouldn't want Warren to start wondering. You never know what it might lead to ... Great intellectual feats, perhaps?'

'Nick off.' She smiled at me.

I waved and pretended to stomp off into the park. See how things were when we were on our own? We could say anything and no one got upset. But when Warren was with us, nothing was funny any more. Melissa went all girlie around him, if you know what I mean. Going all giggly and stupid just because a guy's around is about the most stupid way to waste your time. Melissa was much nicer when she acted like herself. No prizes for guessing what Melissa thought about it. She thought I was imagining things and that when she was with Warren she acted the way she always had. She thought she was just being herself. Well you could've fooled me.

The park was full of dogs and I wished Lucy was with me. Three great danes tore past and nearly knocked me off my feet, leaping all over each other. A bully sat on top of an abandoned picnic bench, keeping a careful eye on one of the joggers, and in the middle of the park on the muddy cricket pitch two bitzers hovered, ready to pounce and play or pounce and fight, depending on which way the wind blew. It was hard to worry about little, unimportant matters like Warren Fitzpatrick when there was so much life in the world. Besides, he was stupid and Melissa was sure to notice it eventually. I was in a position to know, I had to share the physics and chem classroom with him every second day. God knows what he thought he was doing there. His subject selection was obviously the result of a bit of wishful thinking on his parents' part. Sad really, having ambitions for your child and producing something like Warren. In a way it was understandable that Melissa hadn't realised just how dumb he was. Melissa had hardly any classes with him and Warren was the sort of guy who covered up his lack of brains by joking around all the time. If only she knew ...

I reached the end of the park and turned towards home. The sun had struggled out from behind the grey blanket clouds and turned everything to glitter. I squinted at the bright, wet path and thought again about Warren. I had the beginnings of an idea ... It was stupid to let him ruin my life when I knew it was just a matter of time before Melissa woke up to him. Maybe I could move things along a little bit? There couldn't be any harm in that. Besides, I had nothing to do that afternoon, and while the love birds skated, I'd have time to indulge in a little planning ...

In the end, thinking up the ultimate plan to dispose of Warren wasn't all that easy. If you'd asked me what'd be the simplest and best solution, my first inclination would have been to say, shoot him, but that was hardly possible under the circumstances. Besides, there was my commitment to complete non-violence. I won't say my plans were a total waste of time because I enjoyed every minute of them, but I had to confess that spending an entire afternoon thinking about the problem hadn't brought me any closer to a brilliant solution. It wasn't that I couldn't think of anything, it was just that none of my very best plans could be carried out without the active cooperation of several adults — namely our various parents. At the top of my list of possibilities was that Warren's mum or dad would be offered a fantastic job that they couldn't refuse and would decide to move the whole family to Hobart. Since Warren's dad seemed pretty happy running the local used caryard and Warren's mum managed our favourite take away food joint, I didn't think a move to Hobart was realistically on the cards. But if I couldn't move Warren, then maybe I could move me and Melissa? Our parents were always carrying on about how much they'd like to live in the country and since Melissa's dad split a couple of years ago, her mum hadn't been all that happy. We could probably move Melissa's mum but there wouldn't be much point in zooming Melissa and family off to far away places if my parents wouldn't follow — and they wouldn't. Not unless they had some sort of incentive and right now I couldn't think of one. Besides, even if both families could be persuaded to pack up and leave it wouldn't happen in under six months. In six months time Warren would have Melissa so tight around his little finger that she might not even be willing to move when her mum did. I wouldn't put anything past that guy!

That night I dreamt of schemes to get rid of Warren but when I woke in the morning I had to go off to school without having gotten any closer to my ultimate aim. But don't think that I'd given up because I hadn't. Everything still stood as it had the day before: Warren was an idiot, Melissa was a fool blinded by what she imagined was love, and I was determined to rescue my dearest friend from a fate worse than death.

Chapter 2

'**W**here's Melissa?' I asked Warren.

'She must've stayed home.'

'Well that's obvious, isn't it? She hasn't been here all morning which does tend to make you wonder. So what happened?'

'Don't look at me.'

'You're a great help, Einstein. How was she when you left her yesterday?' I pressed him for a decent answer.

'I suppose she was a bit quiet.' He shrugged his shoulders.

'Well, don't kill yourself worrying about her, will you?' I glared at him.

I was spared any further conversation by the beginning of our English lesson. Trouble was, I'd

17

sat next to Warren by accident. Well, not strictly by accident, I'd gone over to speak with him for a couple of minutes and before I knew what was going on the class had started and there wasn't any room for me to move anywhere else. Talk about bad karma!

'Okay,' Mrs Kirkhope peered over her glasses, '*The House that was Eureka*, who's finished it?'

No one put up their hand, the Kirkhope natural law being the more noticeable you were, the more work you were given. I put my head down and looked out of the corner of my eye at Warren who was concentrating deeply on his exercise book and biro. He didn't fool me for a minute.

'And I suppose, since you seem more interested in watching the person sitting next to you than attending to what I'm saying, you're going to tell me you haven't had enough time to finish your reading yet?' Mrs Kirkhope's eyes bored into me.

'Me?'

'Yes you, Miss Sykes,' she smirked at me, 'or am I interrupting your social life?'

Mrs Kirkhope is like that — awful. At least she's awful if you take her too seriously and you don't do any work. I don't mind her all that much because I like reading so I don't have to worry in English.

'Have I read the book?'

'Extraordinary, isn't it?' She invited the rest of the class to join in. 'I've only just asked the class that very question and Miss Sykes isn't sure if that's what we've been talking about. I advise you to listen more closely,' she snarled.

'I've read it,' I said, quickly.

'Well thank you.' She sighed a great sigh of relief. 'And may the class enquire how you found it? Do share with us the benefit of your insight.'

'It was good.' I tried to pull myself together. 'I really enjoyed it. Ah ...' Things were getting uncomfortable. 'What did you think Warren?' I smiled at him, evilly. 'Or perhaps you haven't quite finished it yet?'

'Of course I've finished it.' He glared at me.

'And did you enjoy it?' Mrs Kirkhope leant her weight on to one of the front desks.

'It was all right,' Warren looked around him, uneasily, 'if you're into that sort of thing. I thought the girl was a bit dumb — just sitting around all day and doing nothing.'

'And she had so much choice, didn't she? She couldn't get a job and she had to look after her little sister all the time,' I pointed out.

'Yeah well, you shouldn't get paid for sitting around doing nothing all day — that's what I reckon.'

'Ah ha!' Mrs Kirkhope pounced on him. 'So you're not in favour of unemployment benefits, Warren?'

'I dunno,' he shrugged, 'I guess not — not unless you really deserve them and lots of people just bludge.'

'Oh come on!' Honestly, he made me sick. 'What would you know about it? You've never had to look for work in your life.'

'As a matter of fact I have looked for work. And, more to the point, I've actually worked.' He gave me a filthy look. 'Harder than you ever have, I bet.'

'Let's not let this degenerate into a slanging match between too such close friends,' Mrs Kirkhope said, grinning like a tiger. 'We're talking about unemployment,' she turned to the rest of the class, 'specifically youth unemployment. A subject all of you should be very interested in. So, Warren,' she turned her attention back to him, 'are you hesitant about all government benefits or just benefits for unemployed young people?'

'Both I guess.' Warren shrugged.

'And you, Claire? What's your opinion?' Mrs Kirkhope fixed her eyes on me.

'I just think it isn't right that you get paid less money just because you're younger. You still have to eat and live like unemployed adults.'

'Right!' Mrs Kirkhope clasped her hands together and smiled at us. 'Mr Fitzpatrick and Miss Sykes will be debating the subject of youth unemployment and government benefits in front of the rest of the class this Thursday. Claire,' she looked over at me, 'you will argue in favour of benefits. Warren,' she looked over at the enemy, 'you will be arguing against. You may both absent yourselves from English tomorrow and on Wednesday to prepare your talks and do your research. I expect you to go and visit the Department of Social Security and the Commonwealth Employment Service to get your facts right. The rest is up to you. After you've both addressed the class we will vote on whose talk was the more convincing. A word of warning,' she held up her finger and looked at the class, darkly, 'you will not vote for the speaker whose point of view you happen to share or for the speaker you like more. You will vote for the speaker who argues more convincingly. And just in case you imagine that this is an idle little exercise for the audience, I want you to know that I will be selecting people at random to get up in front of the class and defend their vote in a coherent manner — and I will consider marking your performance. Yes, Warren?' She looked over to where he sat with his hand in the air.

'It's not fair because Claire's got the easiest side. It's not fair if I have to argue against the dole.'

'You should've thought of that before you made your statements about the justice of paying money to people who don't deserve it. Besides,' she waved Warren's complaints aside, 'you're not necessarily arguing against the dole. If I heard you correctly, you're arguing against too liberal a distribution of payment.'

'Oh,' Warren looked mildly confused. 'Yeah, okay. Besides,' he looked over at me, 'it shouldn't be too difficult to top Claire's efforts.'

How about that! Warren wouldn't dream of sneering at me if Melissa was in class. He wouldn't risk spoiling his good guy image. Still, what did I care? The solution to all my problems had landed right in my lap and I hadn't had to do anything to set it up. This way Melissa wouldn't be able to point the finger at me when Warren made a fool of himself in class on Thursday. Normally when Mrs Kirkhope springs one of her little numbers on me, like getting up in front of class and talking, I don't do all that much work beforehand, but this time … This time Warren wouldn't know what'd hit him. I was so happy I sailed through the rest of school. In two days' time I'd be free of Warren and life would go back to how it'd been before he ruined it. It was cause for celebration and I knew exactly who to celebrate with. I'd visit Melissa and make sure she was going to recover from her mysterious illness in time to witness the annihilation of her boyfriend — and I'd buy some treats for us to feast on. Not that Melissa would know what we were celebrating — that could come later after she'd had time to fully recover from splitting up with the creature.

Melissa and I like marshmallows, Twisties, Tim Tams and barbecue flavoured chips. We've sampled just about every sort of junk food on the market, but once you're our age you know exactly what you like. I bought marshmallows at the milkbar because I was sure Melissa would have an open fire if she was sick — her mother thought it cured you faster than anything the chemist could offer — and toasted marshmallows are infinitely better than plain ones. I left the Tim Tams alone in case she was feeling nauseous, but decided that Twisties and barbecue chips could only do her good under the circumstances. Then I did something completely out of character and bought her a bunch of flowers in case she really was too sick to eat. I usually leave the flower buying to the adults, but special occasions call for special treatment.

'Hi.' I poked the flowers ahead of me, around the corner of her bedroom door. 'What's up with you?'

'Oh nothing really,' Melissa said looking grumpy, her hair sticking up on one side like a cockatoo's crest.

'How sick are you? I asked Warren if you were okay but he claimed he didn't know anything about it.'

Melissa sighed. 'Not very. There's nothing really wrong with me. I just didn't want to go to school — and I did have a stomach ache.'

'But not now? Your stomach's all right now?'

'Yeah,' she nodded, 'I'm fine — just bored. You think a day in bed's the only thing in the world that you really want, but staying in bed when there's nothing wrong with you and you've got no one to talk to is the pits.'

'And it does wonders for your looks.' I smiled. 'Seen yourself in the mirror lately?'

'What?' Melissa looked alarmed.

'Lovely hairstyle.'

'For a minute I thought you meant I'd broken out in enormous pimples or something.' She sighed with relief.

'I've brought us something to eat.' I pulled the stuff out of my bag. 'I see your mum's done her bit with the fire.'

'That was the only nice thing,' Melissa agreed, cheering up. 'I like it when it's all windy and rainy outside and you've got a fire in the room with you. How was Warren?'

'Same as usual,' I said, breaking open the marshmallows. 'You sound as though you two have been fighting or something.'

'No.' Melissa shook her head, stabbing viciously at a pink marshmallow with a twig. 'Nothing like that.'

'Could've fooled me.'

'We didn't fight. We never fight. It's just that ...'

'That what?'

'You know how it is.'

'No' I laughed. 'Can't say that I do.'

'He was being a pain, that's all.'

'And it took you this long to notice?' I couldn't keep the smile off my face.

Melissa punched me in the arm. 'I can't talk to you if you'e going to carry on like that. Stop it, okay?'

'Not another word,' I agreed.

She relaxed. 'It was no big deal, I just got annoyed with him.'

'So? Spill the beans. What did he do?'

'I'll tell you if you promise not to take it seriously and not to look happy about it.'

'Cross my heart,' I said, solemnly making a mark over my chest.

'We ran into this mate of his at the rink and all they did is talk, talk, talk about motor racing. It's not that I mind. I mean motor racing is Warren's favourite sport and it's not like I want him to start hating it or anything, it's just that they completely ignored me. For all the attention they paid me I could've been lying dead and bleeding on the ice. It's no big deal, it just annoyed me that's all.'

'I'm not surprised.'

'Yeah I know,' Melissa nodded, 'but then you don't like Warren so anything he does is off as far as you're concerned.'

'Let's leave me out of it then,' I suggested. 'Did you tell him that he ruined your day?'

'He didn't ruin my day,' she sprung to his defence.

'Okay, okay,' I held up my hand. 'Tarnished your day.'

'Yeah.' She grinned and popped a perfectly roasted marshmallow into her mouth.

'So what did he say?'

'If I tell you what he said, you'll just think everything's all his fault.'

'Most people consider loyalty and honesty assets.'

Melissa stretched out her legs and wiggled her toes in front of the fire. 'He just said I was being stupid ...'

'Boy, he can talk,' I snorted.

'See? I can't say anything to you any more.'

'Yes you can, yes you can,' I insisted. 'I promise I won't say another word.'

'Well that's all anyway.' She shrugged. 'Just that he thought I was being a pain and I wasn't. I don't like being ignored and I don't see why they couldn't at least try to include me in their conversation.'

'Yeah, you're right.' I stuffed a handful of Twisties into my mouth and chewed slowly, savoring the taste.

'That's all you've got to say?'

'Ummm.' I nodded, my mouth still full.

'So it's no big deal and I should forget about it?'

'Boy, do you ever read a lot into a person's grunts. There's nothing I can say because you've already told me you don't want to hear anything bad about Warren. But if you really want my opinion, I think it stinks and you were right to get annoyed. After all, you're not just a stuffed doll for him to drag around.'

'Oh he knows that,' she said, quickly.

'See? I told you you wouldn't like it if I said

anything.'

'Let's change the subject.'

Before we got off Warren completely I did tell Melissa about the debate, but I made out that it was a real drag. Melissa might've had a bit of a fight with Warren — and that was all to the good — but I wasn't naive enough to think anything had really changed between them. No, if my plan was going to work I needed Warren to end up looking like a fool while I ended up looking like it'd all happened by accident. But as soon as I'd safely disposed of the business about the debate we got on to more interesting subjects.

It wasn't all that bad getting time off during the next few days to research my talk. What's more I knew I'd done better than Warren because I was smart enough to ring up and ask for appointments before rolling up to the CES and Social Security. When I cruised into Social Security to meet the social worker I saw Warren struggling with the counter staff who only had time to hand him some brochures.

'How's it going?'

'Great,' he said, trying to look cool as he stuffed leaflets into his school bag. 'And you?'

'So-so,' I said, hoping to put him off guard.

'You been down to the CES yet?'

'No. I think I'll leave that for tomorrow. Are

you going there now?'

'Why not? Get it all over and done with. After all, it's not all that complicated, is it?'

'I guess not,' I agreed, hoping I looked like weak competition.

'I'll wait if you like and we can go to the CES together.'

'Ah... No, don't worry,' I said, realising I'd overdone the friendly act. 'I've got to go straight home once I've finished here.'

'Suit yourself.'

He lumbered out the door looking freakish in his school uniform. I think really big guys look strange in uniform. It looks like they're still hanging around school because they've had to repeat so many years. Like they've had to do Year 11 sixteen times or something. Well that's how Warren always looked to me. The worst bit was that Warren thought his size was some sort of winning feature. He even lifted weights to try and make himself look bigger. Guys who lift weights always look like they're wearing a nappy when they walk. Boy, poor Melissa. One day she'd look back on Warren and shudder with embarrassment. But I guess that's the way it is. It's like you can't avoid picking some really weird ones as you go through life. My mum would say it's because there aren't all that many nice men

29

around.

I suppose all this business about Melissa makes me sound like I've never made a mistake in my life? Well, I have. I confess, I went out with the biggest dag in the whole school. We were pretty young then so it wasn't like having a real boyfriend, but all the same we did hold hands and we did kiss. I thought this guy was nice because he was friendly and most of the guys I'd been to primary school with hated girls and wouldn't even talk to us. Well, Greg was friendly all right, but talk about boring! He was so infantile. Greg's idea of a good weekend was to play with his model trains.

I went over to his place to stay once. Mum and Dad let me go because they figured that we were both too young to get into too much trouble. I don't think I was too young, but Greg was. It was a nightmare. I was forced to hang around his parents for company — at least they operated on a more sophisticated level. As soon as I'd been in his house for about ten minutes I knew it just wasn't on, but getting rid of him wasn't easy. It was awful because it wasn't Greg's fault that he was a dag. In fact, the whole time all of this was going on I kept feeling sorry for him — I couldn't stand him, but I couldn't bear to tell him that I couldn't stand him.

I went out with Greg for two weeks after the fatal weekend, just because he looked so happy to see me all the time and telling him to nick off seemed like being mean to a little kid — something I never do. In the end I was a real coward because I wrote him a note and dropped it in his letterbox. Then when he rang I wouldn't come to the phone to talk to him. It took him ages to start speaking to me again. Now we get on really well. He's grown up a fair bit since then.

After Greg, I gave males a rest for a while. One big mistake like that is enough to put you off for life. It wasn't that I didn't like the look of some of the guys I ran across, it was just that any time any of them started to look even vaguely interested I'd panic. What I really couldn't stand was all that business about getting it together in the first place and then immediately realising you didn't like them after all. Then you had to go through the agony of getting rid of them as fast as you possibly could. I used to think that there was something wrong with me because it happened every time I started going out with a guy. I thought Jason was going to be different but he wasn't.

I met Jason when I was fifteen. I'd had a few close shaves with a few different guys before Jason, but I hadn't officially gone out with anyone since that one time with Greg. I met Jason on a riding camp during the summer holidays. I think that part of the reason why we actually ended up going out together was that he wasn't at my school and I didn't think I'd have to worry about him if he turned out to be a dud. In a way Jason wasn't such a dag but he wasn't my type either. On the second night of the camp there was this big bonfire and barbecue. Some of the older kids were drinking beer and fooling around being really stupid so the rest of us sat back a bit in the shadows keeping out of their way. I ended up sitting next to Jason and after a while we started raving. He seemed really easy to talk to and I've always been a sucker for that in a guy. So many guys don't know how to put two words together so when you come across one who can talk to you sensibly for a couple of hours it nearly knocks you off your feet. Well, it sure knocked me off mine. The fact that he was wearing really cool clothes and was kind of nice looking had some effect on me too, but I still think it was the talking that did it.

Nothing happened that night. We raved for a few hours and then the hopeless people who were running the camp turned up and screamed at everyone for letting things get out of hand so we all split to our rooms. I rode next to Jason the next day and then I ended up sitting next to him at dinner time, and again found myself sitting next to him in the television room that night. It was no big deal in the end, he just put his arm around me, and when it got dark and no one could see I put my head on his shoulder to let him know I was into the idea too. So far so good, eh? Trouble was the guy was so full on. While we were still at the camp it didn't seem out of place because practically everyone else had paired off. In fact, sitting in the television room at night you were lucky if you could find anyone actually watching the box. I guess it was a bit revolting really but at the time it seemed cool. No, I didn't mind Jason then, it was when I got back home that things really got under my skin.

Jason would've been the perfect romance if he'd lived at the other end of Tasmania and I'd never seen him again. The trouble was he only lived about ten minutes away from my place and after the camp was over he wanted to carry on like nothing had changed. He came over to my place all the time and kept putting his arm around me and kissing me in front of my parents. I nearly died. It wasn't that my parents are uptight or anything, it was worse than that — they thought it was the funniest thing they'd seen for years. Jason would start up and Mum would start snorting like she had some sort of respiratory complaint. At least Dad had the decency to get out of the room before he packed up laughing. Jason was a bit thick because it didn't matter how many times Mum ended up hiding her head in a cushion and Dad disappeared into the hall, he kept on doing it. I even told him how uncool it was but nothing helped. Finally I ended up literally pushing his arm off me, and then he got into this big huff because I'd hurt his feelings. You can see why I nearly gave up after that. Well, gave up until I met Ivan — the number one passion in my life.

'Hello.' Someone tapped me on the shoulder and I jumped about six feet into the air. 'Sorry, I didn't mean to startle you,' said this bald little squirt of a guy. 'You're... Claire Sykes? Is that right? It's hard to read the writing on this phone message I got.'

'That's right,' I held out my hand, 'I'm Claire.'

'And you wanted to see me about...' He consulted his piece of paper for the second time. 'Ah.' He nodded. 'Applying for the Job Search Allowance. You're still at school at the moment?'

'It's not for me. It's for school — a project I'm doing.'

'Oh,' he said, looking relieved. 'Have you had a look at our brochures?'

'Yes,' I said, hurriedly, 'but I wanted to ask you some questions.'

'I'm not sure how much help I can be.' He tried to edge out of my way but I blocked his exit. 'Ah...Right.' He looked at me, resigned. 'I guess you'd better come into my office. Can I offer you a cup of tea or a biscuit?'

Chapter 3

Warren was doing things by the book. He'd brushed his hair properly — something previously unheard of — he'd put on a clean, ironed uniform, and as he stood up he smiled at the rest of the class. Of course the smile was probably a bad move if the rest of the class felt anything like the way I did about him. Still, there was no denying he was serious about defending his ridiculous opinions. I made myself more comfortable in my seat and looked over at Melissa. Now if I were in Melissa's shoes, I would've been worried. Forget about Warren being Warren, it was enough that Melissa had her boyfriend up in front of the class facing the distinct possibility that he might make a fool of himself. At least with me there wasn't anyone in the room who'd be particularly embarrassed if I blew the whole thing. But Melissa just sat there smiling this mindless smile in Warren's direction — something like, 'Gee you're so wonderful and handsome and I adore being in the same room with you.' I almost found myself thinking that I'd better not win by a landslide because I wouldn't be able to cope with what it'd do to her. That little double take didn't last long mind you — sometimes you've just got to be cruel to be kind. I guess it's something like taking your unsuspecting child to the dentist for their first session under the drill.

'Are you ready, Warren?' Mrs Kirkhope licked her lips in anticipation.

'Yeah.'

'Right then, class.' She rocked back on her heels, relishing the moment. 'Warren will make the opening speech and then we'll hear from Claire. As the second speaker always has the advantage of being able to tailor their talk in response to what they've heard from the first speaker, we'll attempt to balance any unfair advantage by letting Warren and then Claire sum up their positions and respond to any points raised by their opponent. As to your votes,' she grinned, 'this will not be a secret ballot. I want to know who you've voted for so you will put your name at the top of your ballot paper, followed by either Claire's or Warren's name. In the tradition of the real world, Warren and Claire will be allowed to vote for themselves — that is, unless they find themselves overwhelmed by each other's arguments. When you're ready, Warren.' She sat back down in her chair and prepared to listen.

'Right.' Warren cleared his throat and looked around him nervously. 'A lot of kids just leave school and go on the dole because that way they can get more money than what their parents would give them. They sort of reckon that having the money and everything is going to be a real blast and especially if they aren't all that good at schoolwork and everything, then they just leave and don't worry about anything too much. It's different if a kid has to leave school because they're really thick or because their family needs some extra money. If that kid doesn't get a job or gets the sack and they really try to look for more work then the government should give them some help and that' s what the dole is for — only it's not called the dole because they don't want kids to think they're going to get all this money like adults do.'

Warren scratched his head and shuffled his notes around. 'Now with people our age you've got to remember that they've got families and their families should be the ones looking after them, that way the government isn't really the one who should be handing out anything. Besides, unemployed people can't expect the rest of the world to support them in the lap of luxury. Claire obviously hasn't thought about the fact that for every person on the dole — bludger or not — there's some bloke out there working his guts out in a factory or something to support them. It'd be wrong to make the dole too easy to get. Claire wants the government to pay us kids the same money as unemployed adults, she probably even wants the government to go around telling everyone just how to get the money, too — put posters all over the school wall or something.' He snorted out a laugh. 'Well, that's be really great, wouldn't it, Claire? Then you'd have no one at school and hardly anyone who could read or write and they wouldn't thank you for it later. Later when they were a bit older they'd probably try and sue you for running their lives.'

Warren stomped back to his seat.

The class sat still, uncertain for a moment whether he'd really finished. He obviously hadn't blown them away with his brilliance, but no matter how hopeless he was I still had to watch it because Warren was popular with some of the guys in the class. He was especially popular with the sort of guys who weren't all that keen on me. Still, there was nothing much I could do about that — if they couldn't stand me, they wouldn't vote for me, even if I was fifty times better than Warren.

'Thank you, Warren,' Mrs Kirkhope said. 'You can sit back down. Claire,' she beckoned to me with her finger, 'up you come.'

I hadn't been nervous about talking while I sat and listened to Warren make an idiot of himself, but now that I found myself standing in front of all of those faces everything I'd prepared seemed really stupid. I looked around the class hoping for a smile or a nod of encouragement from someone, but they all looked bored to death. 'Yeah, okay,' I cleared my throat. 'So the first thing I want to talk about is the stuff about offering money to anyone who can't find work. After I do that I want to talk about the fact that people our age get paid less than adults when we can't get jobs.'

I could feel my heart pounding inside my chest, but now I'd began I didn't care any more about making Warren look dumb, the only thing I was worried about was getting through my talk without passing out. I told the class about how bad things used to be in the old days and how we had to provide people out of work with a decent amount of money to live on, and then I found myself shuffling my notes just like Warren had. It was really hard to remember what you'd planned to say when you had to do it in front of the thirty people — let alone show off how smart and amusing you were.

'So unemployed people are just like everyone else. They should be given their money and allowed to spend it how they want. Trouble is, if you give people money and let them spend it how they want, and if you don't make things really awful for them then it's true that some people won't want to work. What Warren didn't tell you is that most people don't like being unemployed and it's really unfair to make things hard on them just because there are a few people who bludge. I reckon we shouldn't worry about the bludgers — if there really are any, which there mightn't be anyway.'

I wasn't doing too badly and I knew I'd scored a few points, but I'd done nothing that could be called wiping the floor with Warren. I had to find a way to annihilate him completely. I took a deep breath and got down to it. First I summed up all the points he'd made and took them to extremes. I made him sound like he thought that people of our age shouldn't have any rights at all. Then, when I could feel the class was moving on to my side, I got stuck into the fact that all Warren seemed to talk about was hard-working 'blokes' getting ripped off. I ripped into him about his sexist, male attitudes and when I'd finished, the class actually cheered.

'Thank you, Claire,' Mrs Kirkhope said, giving me a measured look. 'Let's get on with the concluding speeches.'

Warren tried to make up the ground he'd lost but everything he said only made him look worse. I didn't want to overdo it, so once he'd stepped down I kept my response low key. I stuck to the facts — pointing out how people under eighteen were discriminated against — and left the rest up to the class. I had to admit I had a few anxious moments while Mrs Kirkhope counted the votes, but I needn't have worried. I won easily.

'Be quiet!' Mrs Kirkhope instructed. 'The question is, who's going to be first to defend their vote?'

I didn't listen all that carefully to what everyone had to say. Usually I would've been really into it, but all I could think about was what was going on in Melissa's head. I was so sure that beating Warren was going to work, but now I'd done it, it was hard to tell. As soon as the bell went for lunch I headed for the door. Melissa was right behind me.

'Thank God that's over,' I sighed. 'What a drag.'

'Personally I thought it was awful.'

'I guess so. Pretty boring stuff really, but someone had to win.'

'I hope you're happy now. I hope it was worth it.'

'What do you mean?' I turned around to face her.

'Exactly what I said. I hope you're satisfied.' She looked at me coldly and stepped past me into the toilets, swinging the door behind her.

'Melissa!' I followed her in. 'Wait.'

The bathroom was packed and Melissa shut herself in a cubicle before I could get hold of her. Not the nicest place to sort something out with a friend. I had to hang around pretending I was fixing my hair while I waited. Banging on locked doors doesn't do a whole lot for your image — at least not in my school it doesn't. About ten minutes later Melissa came out, washed her hands and walked straight past me.

'Hang on!' I said, chasing after her.

But guess who was standing patiently out in the hall — yep, dear, old Warren. I slowed down

43

and acted like nothing much was going on.

'Come on, Warren,' Melissa said, without looking in my direction, 'let's get out of here.'

I know when I'm not wanted and I know for sure when I've stuffed things up, so I took the hint and left the two of them alone. There were plenty of other people to hang around with and for a while I tried to convince myself it was no big deal — that Melissa would cool off after a couple of hours and things would go back to normal again. I mean, it wasn't as if I'd really done anything except beat her precious Warren in class and who cared about that? She had to be nuts if she thought I was going to let him win just because he was her boyfriend. She'd hardly expect him to do the same for me, so what was the big deal? A couple of other people noticed I was getting the treatment from her and let me tell you they weren't all that impressed. If I didn't know Melissa was worth the effort I think I would have left it at that and found someone else to be friends with. As it was I didn't try to speak to her that day. I figured she'd have recovered within a day or so, so what was the point? Only trouble was, when I rolled up at school the next day it was the same old thing again. By Saturday morning I was beside myself and Mum didn't help matters any.

'Funny Melissa hasn't called yet. I can't think of the last time you two missed your usual Saturday morning gossip.'

'We do not gossip! Why do you have to be so rude about everything I do?'

'Okay, okay, she held up her hands protectively, 'only making conversation. Besides, there's nothing wrong with gossiping.'

'So you say.'

'My, aren't we touchy this morning? Anything in particular? Have you got your period or something?'

'Do you have to?' I gave her a look. 'When did I last enquire about your bodily functions? Maybe you'd like to give me a full run down. I didn't realise this was such a "sharing" family.'

'Ouch!' She pretended to hold up a burnt finger. 'Think I'll go and read in another room.'

You couldn't even have a decent fight in my family. Start stirring things and Mum and Dad would just smile and leave the room. My brother was the only one you could really brawl with and he'd left home to live with his girlfriend. I thought about going around there and starting an argument. Well, not really but I wished there was someone I could let it all out on. I couldn't stand sitting around the house burning up with no one to talk to and nothing to do. I tried reading but all I found myself doing was acting out these long arguments with Melissa inside my head. I tried listening to music but that was no better. I got my diary out and wrote all these rude things about Warren and that helped a bit, but it didn't do a whole lot to stop Melissa giving me the silent treatment. Finally I even tried looking at things from her point of view — something I never enjoy doing — but I still couldn't work out what I'd done that was so bad. After all, she didn't know what my secret plans had been. As far as she knew it was just an ordinary class exercise. Besides, when you debate something you're *meant* to make the other person look stupid — you're supposed to win. I shrugged my shoulders and decided to go out for a while.

I walked up to the park keeping my eyes on the pavement so I wouldn't have to smile at anyone. I kicked viciously at the leaves on the concrete and when I got into the park I kicked the grass. Juvenile I know, but I had to do something. I sat down on one of the benches and stared gloomily at the oval. It was covered with all the usual fanatics jogging around trying to defy old age. I get a bit worried about the ones who look like they're going to keel over and have a heart attack — you know, the fat ones who run around making their faces turn purple. Of course there were healthier types too. I could see a couple of girls from school working out and three guys from my class kicking a footy around. Then out of the corner of my eye I saw them — Melissa and Warren.

Melissa was wearing shorts and an old T-shirt. Warren was rugged up like he was about to step out onto the snow. I wondered what on earth they were up to. I even got so far as to stand up and start walking in their direction, then I thought better of it. If I was going to talk to Melissa I wasn't going to do it in front of Warren, and I wasn't going to do it on the run. They jogged slowly around the track, not talking to each other, just concentrating on keeping in step. Then they started on their second lap and I lost sight of them as they took the path that led under the old Cypress trees. I wondered what Melissa was up to. Melissa had always been fairly cool about active sports. I played a fair bit of netball, loved athletics, and I swam a lot, but Melissa had never been all that interested in anything that required effort. I wondered how long she'd last. I guessed she'd manage about another lap and a half if she was really determined. I waited, my eyes trained on where the path re-emerged from the trees, and sure enough they jogged back into sight, rounding the picnic area and passing a group of older health fanatics before entering the straight right beneath my perch on the hill. Below my seat Melissa gave Warren a pat on the shoulder and slowed to a walk.

'Catch you later,' I heard her say as she stopped and bent over to regain her breath.

Here was my chance. Warren had increased his pace and was well out of earshot and there was nothing to stop me going down and sorting things out. Still, I couldn't make myself move. Melissa stood up and looked straight at me. I smiled but didn't wave. It was hard to think of carrying on with our fight but I didn't know how she felt. After all, she hadn't rung that morning like she usually did. But then she gave me a wave and I felt relief sweep through me. It's weird the way an argument with your best friend can ruin your life completely. I waved back and she started up the hill towards me coming to rest, hot and tired, on the bench beside me.

'Forgiven me, have you?' I asked hopefully, forgetting that I'd decided I hadn't done anything wrong.

'Maybe.' She wiped the sweat off her face with the back of her arm. 'Although you were a creep.'

'Me? What did I do?'

'Just hung it all over Warren for no reason.'

'It was just a debate.'

'Pull the other one.'

'It was,' I insisted.

'You went out of your way to make out he was some sort of right wing, fascist, macho man. Don't tell me you didn't.'

'Yeah but —'

'But nothing,' she said, firmly. 'Admit it, you were doing your best to make a fool of him, and you had your own devious reasons for doing it.'

'Do I have to?'

'If you want me to keep talking to you, you do.'

'Well all right,' I agreed, 'but what's so bad about that?'

'What's so bad about that?' She looked at me, amazed. 'You stand up there mouthing off about how people should be able to make their own decisions and not be treated like belongings and you get around treating me like you know what's best for me. You've sure got a nerve.'

'Sorry,' I shrugged lamely. 'I guess I just got carried away.'

'That's a polite way of putting it. Knowing you, you probably planned it, from start to finish, but let's not go into that. I'm still too annoyed with you to want to make things any worse. Let's just say we agree to disagree where Warren's concerned and you'll promise not to go

49

interfering in my life any more?'

'Okay.'

'I wish I could believe you.' She sighed. 'Trouble is I've known you for years and in my experience, that little brain of yours just keeps on ticking over.'

'No, no.' I shook my head. 'Cross my heart and hope to die. I won't hassle you about Warren ever again.'

Chapter 4

I was as good as gold for the next four weeks. I smiled politely at Warren whenever he came anywhere near me and I kept my mouth closed. To tell you the truth I was serious about letting the whole thing drop and putting up with Warren until Melissa got tired of him herself. I was serious about it until halfway through my fourth week of model behaviour, then everything got out of hand again. And it was all Warren's fault. Warren and his ego. I'd gone down to watch the footy with Melissa because our school was playing in the semi-finals and Warren was team captain. Let me straighten things out a little so you don't get the wrong impression. I've never liked football. If I'm going to watch sport I'll watch something that doesn't involve a whole lot of people getting together and gouging each other's eyes out. Something like squash or tennis. Even basketball isn't that bad if you have to watch something. But Warren was a footballer — not that surprising really considering what he was like. But let me get back to the story. Melissa wanted to watch Warren play, I didn't want to hang around on my own at home, the weather wasn't all that bad, and at least Warren would be down on the field while we watched — all in all it didn't seem such a bad idea, so I decided to trail along.

Melissa and I got together something to eat, grabbed a rug to sit on, put on our sunnies, packed our books in case things got boring, and headed off feeling good. It took us about twenty minutes to get to the oval and although there were a few car loads of parents barracking for their little darlings, the grandstand was fairly empty. Not entirely empty unfortunately. Down by the rail there were about fifteen, hard-core football groupies. Some of the girls were in our year at school, but there were quite a few younger ones there too, drooling over the guys running around the oval splattered in mud. I ask you, is a smelly mud-covered guy really worth the effort? The groupies certainly seemed to think so. Some of the girls were going out with guys on the team, but it was amazing how many others were prepared to sit there wasting their weekend for no good reason. I watched Warren and the others play for about fifteen minutes and then grabbed my book and lost myself in the story I was reading. About halfway through two of the groupies climbed up between the seats and interrupted our peace.

Janet flicked back her long red hair and smiled at us. 'Hi,' she said.

'Hi,' I agreed, and pointedly put my head back in my book.

'Look we've been talking,' Janet nodded towards the other groupies, 'and we think we should do something really special for the finals.'

I looked at Melissa out of the corner of my eye and we bit our lips, trying not to smile. Melissa and I have never been into doing group stuff — especially on behalf of a whole lot of guys who get too much attention anyway.

'Ah ... We're not really interested.' I shook my head as kindly as I could.

'But it's our big chance to win this year,' the second girl pleaded. 'We really want the guys to know we're behind them all the way.'

'Speak for yourselves,' I said.

'Come on, Claire.' Janet rolled her eyes. 'I know you're not interested but don't spoil it for Melissa. Melissa's going out with the team captain, maybe she wants to do something for the team. I mean morale counts and if we're going to win, then we have to put some effort into it. After all, the guys have to get up early every morning for training, the least we can do is organise something for the day.'

'Oh my heart bleeds.' I clutched my chest. 'Honestly,' I shook my head, 'you lot are really warped. When's the last time the guys came down and did something special for our netball finals? Next time I see them running around in cute little shorts, singing cute little songs on our behalf, I'll let you know.'

'Yeah I know, but all the same ...' Melissa said, starting to look sheepish.

'Go on,' I said, icily.

'Well, Janet's right about the finals being special. Not just for the guys in the team,' she added, hurriedly, 'but for the rest of the school too.'

'Let me put your minds at ease on that last point. The majority of the school population couldn't care less what happens in the finals.'

'Well they should care,' Janet said. 'Maybe if we do something special this year we can get a whole lot of new supporters?'

'That's a point,' Melissa agreed. 'What did you

have in mind?'

Janet and the other girl glanced in my direction and looked uncomfortable.

'Don't mind me,' I said. 'Just pretend I'm not here.'

'Well,' Janet said, still eyeing me uneasily, 'we all think it'd be really fun to do some sort of aerobics thing at the start and we might even be able to get Ms Gibbs to choreograph something special for us.'

'I knew it,' I groaned. 'Cheerleaders. Have you no shame?'

'What's so bad about that?' Janet's offsider asked.

'If you don't know already, I'm not going to waste my breath trying to educate you on the finer points of exploitation.'

Janet and her friend looked at each other and snickered.

'Leaving Claire's neurosis aside,' Janet looked at Melissa, 'what do you think?'

'If all of you want to do it, I guess I should be in it too. I mean it'd look pretty bad if I was the only girlfriend not doing anything.'

'Okay then.' Janet looked pleased. 'We're going to meet at lunch on Monday in the gym. We'll see you there.' They wandered off and left us alone again.

'Don't say anything,' Melissa said.

'I don't have to. Let's just say it's hard to resist the pressure to do the girlfriend bit.'

'Well it is.'

'Exactly.'

My only hope was that our team would lose and wouldn't get to play in the finals at all. That last hope turned to dust as I watched them romp home and win the match. I guess luck just wasn't on my side. But I didn't say anything to Melissa. No not a word on the subject of dancing girls and female exploitation. What had changed was my decision to keep out of Melissa's affairs. She'd said that it was her life — and it was — but I owed her some loyalty. After all, if your friend is drowning you hold out your hand and save her, don't you?

As it was I had plenty of encouragement from Ivan, my occasional boyfriend. Ivan and I had been friends for ages and in the last year or so we'd been going out together whenever we got the chance — which wasn't all that often because Ivan and his dad had moved to Hobart and Ivan only appeared when he was visiting his mum. Ivan's mum was a bit of a rebel. I suppose you could say she was an example of someone who was old but who didn't do the sort of things people expected her to do. Ivan didn't live with his dad because he chose to, or because his father won custody of him when he was little, he lived with his dad because his mum packed up and left him there. She just decided she'd rather be on her own. Now that Ivan was older he could probably go and live with her if wanted to. I mean she wouldn't mind having him around, but he was pretty happy with his dad. When his dad decided to move to Hobart Ivan could've gone to live with his mum, but he didn't want to — which is why we ended up having such a weird, part-time relationship. When he first left I think we both thought it was pretty well all over between us, but then he kept coming back to visit in school holidays and we'd just take up where we left off. Maybe it would've been different if either of us had met up with someone else, but we never did. Well … Maybe once or twice I might've come close to starting something with someone at school, but nothing ever came of it. I left Melissa and Warren after the match and returned home to find Ivan sitting reading a book on my front door step.

'Ivan! Boy, am I ever glad to see you.' I pushed his book aside and threw myself on to his lap. 'You didn't say you were coming. I had no idea.'

'Neither did I.' He smiled and put his arms around me. 'Dad's sick and I decided to come and stay with Mum for the duration.'

'Boy, I'm glad to see you.'

'You already said that.' He kissed me.

'Because it's true.'

'So what's new?' he asked.

'Plenty,' I said. 'Come inside and I'll fill you in.'

We went up to my room and got settled. That's the thing about Ivan, I wouldn't see him for months on end and then he'd appear and it'd feel as though it was only a day or so since we'd last been together. I gave him a great, long kiss and then began to explain about Melissa and Warren. Ivan knew Warren and he looked really shocked.

'Maybe we could poison him,' he suggested, without any prompting on my part.

'A man after my own heart.' I gave him a hug. 'No, I'm into realism, remember? Besides, I already thought of that ages ago. Think of something original.'

'But poison's such an efficient and direct method.'

'It's not that I haven't been seriously tempted, but ... '

'He's really into sport, isn't he?'

'Well what did he talk about the last time you spoke to him?'

'I never spoke to him. When I was at school I hung out with you and Melissa.'

'But you must've noticed what he was like.'

'Let's just say I'm not all that surprised to hear he's not your type. What does Melissa see in him?'

'How about his body? I have to admit he's pretty gorgeous looking, and even Melissa isn't immune to pure lust.'

'Are they sleeping together?' Ivan pricked up his ears.

'None of your business.'

'She hasn't told you, has she?'

'None of your business,' I repeated.

'No,' he looked at me, thoughtfully, 'she hasn't told you, but you think she is. Otherwise you wouldn't be looking so annoyed with me for asking.'

'Nick off.'

'Right,' he cleared his throat and tried to look serious, 'back to my question. He loves sport?'

'Do mice love cheese? Do duck shooters love guns? Do vegetarians love rhubarb? Need you ask?'

'And Melissa's still the lazy sloth she always was?'

'Yep,' I agreed. 'Apart from the occasional run around the park, I'd have to say she was, and still is, a slug.'

'That's it then.' Ivan smiled in triumph. 'All we

have to do is build up the sporting angle and drive Melissa crazy. Either she'll take up drinking or she'll ditch young Warren.'

'Possible, possible.' I murmured to myself, thinking over our chances. 'Hey, how about this? It's Melissa's birthday soon, why don't we steer Warren towards a suitable present.'

'Like what? A year's subscription to the local gym? Colour coordinated jogging gear?'

'No...' I leaned back against Ivan and stretched my arms up around his neck. 'I was thinking more along the lines of an outing. A special treat.'

'You're so wicked, Claire.' He pinched me. 'I pity poor Melissa.'

'And you're not, I suppose?'

'Why do you think we get on so well? We're two of a kind. So what's it to be? Night cricket's no good — wrong season.'

'Boxing,' I suggested. 'Now there's a sport no one with any sensitivity could learn to love.'

'Possible, but I'm not sure even Warren could be persuaded that Melissa would kill for a night ring side. We want something that'd seem natural coming from Warren. What's his favorite sport?'

'Motor racing!' I started to laugh as I pictured the possibilities. 'Oh wow, Ivan, we've done it this time. I mean, could there be a more tedious pastime than sitting on your bum watching cars go around and around in circles? And I know Melissa agrees with me because they had a fight about it only recently.'

Ivan nodded his head, thoughtfully. 'I've got to admit motor racing rates pretty low on the scale of human achievement.'

'Now all we have to do is sow the seed with Warren. And I know just the person to do it.'

'Oh no!' Ivan tried to slip out from under my arms.

'Come on, Ivan, that's not the way to behave.' I slid him down on the couch and sat on him so he couldn't move. 'You haven't seen me for at least a month and already you're letting me down. Where's your love and adoration? You're supposed to worship the ground I walk on.'

'Well I do — sort of.' He made a face and struggled to escape.

'So it's a deal,' I said quickly. 'Now down to more pleasurable matters.' I lay down on top of him. 'How long are you staying with your mum?'

'I'm not sure. It depends on how long Dad stays sick.'

'Would it be wrong to hope for a long drawn-out illness? It's nothing too serious, is it?'

'Not life threatening. About a month's worth of indisposition, I'd say.'

'So you'll be coming to school?'

'Yeah.' Ivan looked less than pleased at the thought. 'In fact I may have to stay for the rest of the year. Dad doesn't want me moving around when I should have my head in my books.'

'Great. Just think of the passionate moments we can have down behind the bicycle shed ...'

'Hey, steady on, Claire,' he complained. 'The bicycle shed's a bit public, isn't it?'

'Holding hands in assembly?' I suggested.

'Possible.'

'How about sleeping over at my place?'

'Would your parents let me?' He looked interested.

'No, but it's a nice idea, isn't it?'

'Wonderful.'

'There's no one here now,' I pointed out.

'True ...'

The rest of the story is censored — sorry. Ivan and I didn't see each other enough as it was so we had to protect the time we had together. Let's just say we got about two hours on our own before Mum and Dad came back. Unfortunately, Mum wasn't exactly tickled pink to find Ivan at home.

Mum and I have got a deal going about my marks at school being good enough to get me into engineering and she detests anything that could get in my way — Ivan included. She thinks he's a nice guy and everything, but she also thinks guys are a nuisance when you've got a lot of work to do. She says I'm her and Dad's superannuation so they have to take me seriously. Lots of jokes float around our house about how Mum and Dad are just waiting for me to get it together so they can retire in peace and live off my earnings. Fat chance, I always told them. I was going to make mega bucks by designing radical, non-polluting industrial machinery, and I wasn't about to give them a cent.

Well, that was version number six hundred and seventy-four in how Claire Sykes would conquer the world. At least I wasn't mean minded. A least I wasn't planning a future selling nightwear in the local department store. There sure were some deadly jobs around. Take stocking machine operator. Or petrol pump assistant. My absolute favourite — that I put down as my number one career selection on every vocational guidance questionnaire we got at school — was working for directory assistance at Telecom. Now there was a wild job if ever I saw one. Imagine sitting there all day, clicking away at the computer, looking up people's phone numbers. I was devastated when I heard they were thinking of fully computerising the system. It looked like I was going to have to strike that one off my list. Melissa was another story. She wanted to go and live overseas — which is why she wanted to be a teacher. Personally, I couldn't stand it. I hate kids.

'Claire. Claire!' Dad stood and glared at me, hands on hips.

'What?'

'I've just invited Ivan for dinner and I was asking you whether you wanted to have Melissa and what's-his-name over too.'

'No way! Invite Warren here? You've got to be kidding, Dad.'

'But hang on.' Ivan made a meaningful face at me. 'Don't you think it'd be a good idea to ask him over?'

'No I don't.'

'Think, Clarie. Upstairs, a few hours ago, remember? Ring any bells?'

'Oh yeah.' I nodded in his direction before turning to Dad. 'What a great idea. I'll ring Melissa now. What time shall I tell them to come?' I asked Dad.

'But you just said you didn't want them.' Dad looked confused.

'Yes, but I've changed my mind,' I explained, patiently.

Ivan disappeared to square things with his mum and left me suffering in the kitchen with

Dad. I tried to creep away, but you know what parents are like — eagle eyes when it comes to catching you avoiding your fair share of the housework. I told Dad that I really should've been up in my room making myself glamorous for the evening ahead, but he said that since I'd never been very interested in make-up and clothes, he wasn't at all convinced glamour was called for, let alone possible, under the circumstances. He was so rude. My father had no idea how a proper dad was supposed to behave. Number one, fathers were supposed to dote on their daughters, and my dad just wasn't interested. Not that he was horrible or anything — I'm not saying that. He just wasn't the sort of father who wanted to spend hours listening to all your problems or telling you how clever you'd been or even admiring how hard you'd tried. Dad was the sort of person who presumed everything was fine. In other words he never paid much attention to anyone — except maybe our dog whom he was convinced suffered from an insecurity complex. I mean, what sort of a parent sends a sick child to school and coddles an obese golden retriever? My sort, that's who.

The dinner went off okay. At first I thought it was going to be a real disaster because Mum and Dad had obviously decided to 'show an interest' in all of us, which ended up being more like a mass interrogation than a conversation. Mum and Dad can rustle up a conversation with me when they're put into a tight spot and can't avoid it, but sit them around a table with a few sixteen and seventeen year olds and it's question time. The only trouble is, the questions only seem to go in one direction — from them to us.

They spent the evening grilling Ivan about his father's illness, Warren about small business in a recession, Melissa about her ambitions, and me about my opinion on micro-economic reform. And my parents call that talking! Things only broke up when Ivan got talking to Melissa and I made a supreme effort and raved with Warren. After that, Mum and Dad had no choice but to spend the rest of the evening talking to each other, clearing the plates, and doing the washing up. I only hoped that somehow Ivan would manage to say something to Warren. If he didn't get him on his own soon, he'd probably make his own arrangements for Melissa's birthday and our best chance would be lost.

Chapter 5

'**I** can't believe it!' Melissa stormed into the sitting-room. 'I just can't belieive it! Imagine the sort of brain it takes to come up with such a warped notion.'

'What, or whom, are we talking about?' I asked.

'Warren, that's who.' She threw herself into a chair. 'Do you know what that idiot has gone and done?'

'Are we talking about the same Warren? The only Warren I know, is "darling Warren" with the body of a Greek god.'

'That's him.'

'There must be something wrong with my ears.' I banged the side of my head with the palm of my hand.

'Shut up, Claire. You're such a pain sometimes. Now is not the moment to make fun of my love life. "Love life," what a phrase.' She sighed and hit the arm of her chair with her fist. 'I can't believe I've actually been wasting my time on someone who's got no idea what's important to me — what *I* like. I know all about him. I know what he likes to eat, what he likes to talk about, who his friends are, where he lived when he was a little kid — I even know the name of the pet chicken he had when he was four years old. And what does he know about me? Nothing, zero, zilch. One girlfriend's as good as the next to him. Typical male! I made the mistake of thinking he was worth the effort. What an idiot I've been. What a total idiot.

'Ah ... And this revelation has come about because ... ?'

'Because of my birthday. Do you know what that imbecile did?'

I shook my head and tried to ignore the hot flushes of guilt I was experiencing.

'He bought me the complete Metalica collection.

'The complete Metalica collection?' I repeated, dumbly.

'You heard.'

'But I don't understand — '

'*You* don't understand. What about me? I'm the one he bought it for. Imagine how confused I feel.'

'But you hate Metalica.'

'Exactly. That's just my point.'

I shook my head. 'That's weird.'

'And they're compact discs.' Melissa started pulling angrily at the loose threads on the couch.

'But you don't have a CD player.'

'No need to remind me. Maybe he hasn't noticed?' She looked at me seriously. 'I mean, what's wrong with him? How could he possibly have thought that I, me, Melissa, would want the complete Metalica CD collection for my seventeenth birthday — even if I did have a player to play it on. I've always hated Metalica. I hate that sort of music.'

'I know.'

'The question is, why doesn't he know?'

'Look, maybe he made an honest mistake.'

'Read 'idiotic' for 'honest' and you might be right,' she seethed.

'Does he like Metalica?'

'I suppose so.' She shrugged. 'I mean, I guess so. I can't think why else he'd buy it.'

'Did you ask him?'

'No, of course not. I was too mad to ask him anything. I was speechless. What can you say to

69

soemone like that?'

'Don't ask me.' I made a face. 'So what are you going to do?'

'Drop him.' She thumped the poor chair for the second time.

'Really?'

'Of course. We're completely incompatible. We've got nothing in common.'

'Well, I've never thought so, but ... '

'I think I got carried away with the idea of going out with someone who was a real guy's guy,' she mused. 'You know what I mean, someone who hung around with all the other guys and looked like he knew what he was doing?'

'Well, I suppose so ... '

'No, you wouldn't understand.' She waved away the possibility. 'You've never been attracted to guys with a real macho image.'

'Right.' I nodded, deciding it was probably best to agree with everything she said.

'Trouble is, you don't know that they're not worth the effort until you've given them a try. And he was beautiful — you have to admit that?' She looked at me hopefully.

'One of the best looking guys at school. Hey listen, I forgot to say happy birthday. So Happy Birthday.'

'Thanks.' Melissa rested her chin on to her hands, and looked glum.

'Do you want your present now?'

'Give it to me later when I'm in a better mood.' She waved me back into my seat. 'You know what?'

'What?'

'I'm going around there now to ditch him. I don't want to go out with that creep for a minute longer than I have to.' She stood up and pulled her coat back on. 'I'll be back,' she called out over her shoulder. 'Wait here because I'll be back in about ten minutes.'

As soon as I heard the front door slam shut, I raced to the phone. Maybe Ivan hadn't exactly followed our plan, but he'd certainly done the trick — he'd discovered how to get rid of Warren. I waited for someone to pick up the phone, but it just rang and rang. Of course it didn't matter all that much that Ivan wasn't home. I didn't need to talk to him — we could have a long gossip about the details later — but all the same it was frustrating having to hang around waiting for Melissa's return without anyone to talk to in the meantime.

I wandered into the kitchen and made myself a peanut butter and strawberry jam sandwich with far too much butter. I carried it back into the

71

sitting-room where there was a fire in the grate. Our house was old and cold. It was a big wooden, two-storey place without any central heating, and in winter you really couldn't sit around unless you were in a room where there was a fire. At night I used to run from the bathroom, where there was a bar heater up on the wall, and jump into my bed like I was in the Olympics or something. It was icy cold when your legs first hit the sheets and you had to clutch on to your hotwater bottle for dear life, but it was worse if you got in slowly. And infinitely worse if you made yourself walk slowly across the cold, bare floorboards. When I got my own place, every bed in it was going to have an electric blanket, and there'd be wall to wall carpet in every room. Better still, I'd go and live in the tropics where all you had to worry about was the heat — well, the heat and the insects.

I pulled my feet up underneath me, rested my homework on my knees and began munching on my sandwich. Of course there wasn't much point in trying to work when Melissa would be back from Warren's house at any moment, pounding on my front door, but I thought I should give it a try. Besides, it usually took more than ten minutes to break up with someone. Warren would probably be trying to persuade her to give him another chance. It was hard to imagine Warren down on his knees weeping into Melissa's lap — in fact, it was gross. Probably he wouldn't weep. I'd never seen anything in Warren remotely resembling a personality, but since he was human he had to have feelings, so he'd have to be upset about them splitting up. I'd ask Melissa about it when she got back. I'd have to be tactful though because she'd probably be upset after talking to him. Still, it'd be interesting to find out exactly how Warren had reacted to being dropped.

I leant over the arm of the couch and carefully lowered my plate on to the rug. My fingers were sticky from the oozing jam and, not having anything suitable to wipe them on, I had to lick them clean. It wasn't the most attractive sight in the world, but I had a library book on my lap and I didn't think I'd be popular if I returned it re-decorated, compliments of the Sykes' kitchen. I looked at my watch. She'd been gone for twenty minutes so she wouldn't be long. Still, it was better to read than just sit and wait. At first it was hard to concentrate and my eyes slid over the text without taking anything in, but after a bit I got absorbed. I was doing some research for a physics assignment and since physics was my favourite subject, I didn't mind reading about time and space and all of that sort of stuff. It was only when the room became too dark for me to see the book that I realised a couple of hours had passed and there was still no sign of Melissa. I ventured out into the cold of the hallway and picked up the phone. I wouldn't ring Warren's house — too embarrassing — but I'd ring Mellissa's in case she'd been too upset to walk all the way over to my place. Her mother answered the phone.

'No, Claire, she's not in.'

'Oh,' I said lamely, wondering what my next move should be. 'I suppose she's probably still at Warren's then. I was expecting her over here.'

'Well I don't think she'll be coming tonight. It's her birthday remember. She and Warren have got a big night out planned.'

'No that's all off,' I explained. 'She was definitely coming over here when I spoke to her a couple of hours ago.'

'In that case she must have changed her mind again, Claire, because she was in and out of here about fifteen minutes ago, getting changed. If it's really important I suggest you call her at Warren's place. You might still catch them if you're lucky.'

'Are you sure?' I asked.

'Of course. Is something the matter, dear?' Melissa's mother asked. 'You sound worried.'

'Oh no.' I shook my head quickly as though she

was standing there watching me. 'No, nothing — everything's fine.'

'Shall I leave a message for her? I could if you like — although I don't expect her back early.'

'No don't worry. Thanks anyway.'

Thank God I had some distraction lined up for the rest of the evening because there was nothing more unbearable than a mystery — well, for me there wasn't. All I could think of was that Warren had somehow managed to persuade Melissa to spend one last night with him before they called it quits. Or maybe Melissa had gone all weak at the knees and decided to wait until after their evening out before she sent him packing. After all, they'd already booked everything and Melissa hated wasting money — especially her own. It sounded plausible, but I still couldn't work out why she hadn't called me or dropped by to let me know what was going on. I stomped around my room for a while, trying to figure it all out, but I was saved from too much agony by the arrival of the family — practically every member of it. Mum, Dad, my brother and his girlfriend, my cousin Caroline, my aunt and uncle, and I were all expected over at my grandmother's house for dinner. At least I'd managed to wangle an invitation for Ivan — grand family dinners are easier to bear when you've got someone with you who's on your side and understands who everyone is and what they're on about.

'Claire, you're not ready yet.' Mum glared at me. 'Do you know what time it is?'

I looked at my watch. 'Six-fifteen.'

'And?' She nodded her head like a little bird. 'And?'

'And what?' I asked.

'I told her, didn't I, Gordon?' Mum looked at Dad. 'Didn't I tell her this morning that she had to be dressed and ready to go by six?'

Dad nodded absently at Mum as he struggled to get the dog's leash clipped on to her collar.

'We're not bringing *her* with us, are we?' My brother stood by the open front door, looking appalled. 'She smells and drops hair all over the seat. Leave her behind, Dad — have some sense for once.'

'Granny loves to see Poppet and Poppet enjoys the trip. It wouldn't be fair to leave her here on her own while the rest of the family go out and enjoy themselves.'

'She's not *in* the family. I'm not related to a dog if you don't mind. She's a pet, Dad — a pet.' My brother rolled his eyes in his girlfriend's direction.

'Upstairs.' Mum turned her attention back to me. 'Quick, we're going to be late. By the way, you did tell Ivan we'd pick him up, didn't you?'

'Yeah of course,' I agreed, 'but why can't I go like this? There's nothing wrong with these jeans — they're new.'

'Look,' Mum sighed, 'your grandmother expects everyone to get dressed up when we come for dinner. You know that. And for Granny, dressed up means slacks or a dress.'

'Slacks.' I put my finger down my throat as though I needed to vomit. 'I wouldn't be seen dead in slacks.'

'She's all right as she is, Lyn,' my aunt said to Mum. 'Mother should be pleased to see us, not worrying about what we're all wearing. Besides, we'd better get going if we're going to get there on time. Who's coming in our car?'

'We are,' my brother said, pulling his girlfriend as far away from Poppet and Dad as he could.

'You two went with Aunty Nancy and Uncle Peter last time,' I complained. 'This time you get Poppet, and Ivan and I ride in style.'

'Aunty Nancy and Uncle Peter don't want to play chauffeur to you and your little boyfriend,' my brother sneered at me.

'Says who?'

'Just go and get in the car,' Dad said, holding the end of Poppet's leash for me to take hold of. 'We know where Ivan lives so it's less trouble for us to pick him up than it is for Nancy and Peter. Take Poppet out to the car while I lock up.'

'Did you give her a car sickness tablet?' I asked. 'I'm not getting in the car with her if she's going to throw up all over me again.'

'She doesn't get sick any more,' Dad announced as he disappeared down the hallway towards the back of the house.

'Bull!' I called out after him.

'Just go and get in the car.' Mum began pushing me out the door after the others. 'I'll get some towels just in case.'

'Poppet goes in the front,' I insisted as Mum returned. 'She can sit on Dad's lap. I'm not having her in the back with me and Ivan. She'll throw up. She always throws up.'

'All right,' she gave in, 'she can sit with your father. But you'd better stop complaining — and don't fight with your brother. You know how Granny hates it when you do that.'

'I never fight with him,' I pointed out, 'he always fights with me.'

'Whatever,' Mum agreed, climbing into the driver's seat.

Mum put the keys into the ignition and we waited tersely for Dad to finish turning out all the lights, and checking all the doors and windows.

'I just hope Ivan's ready,' Mum said, as Dad

lifted Poppet gently on to his lap.

'Ivan's never late, is he, Poppet?' He gave the dog an unnecessary pat on the head.

We zoomed over to Ivan's house in silence. It was always like this when we went to visit my granny for dinner. My parents are tolerable on their own, but they go to pieces when they have to front up to the rest of the relatives.

Ivan got some points from Mum because he was waiting near the front door and he wasn't wearing jeans, and Dad was rapt because Ivan was a big enough suck to say hello to Poppet as he climbed in beside me. Personally, I didn't mind how much he sucked up to my parents so long as he had enough brains not to agree with Dad's suggestion that Poppet would be much more comfortable in the back seat with us. But Ivan's no fool. He told Dad that Poppet would feel safer sitting next to her master. It was like music to my father's ears.

The drive to my granny's takes about an hour. She lives on a farm by herself and we go there once a month to visit and check that she's all right. She always cooks these huge, greasy roast dinners which everyone hates eating. Not her fault really, I suppose. Mum reckons that's the sort of stuff they used to eat all the time when she was a kid. In fact, her dad used to go out and kill a sheep whenever they needed any meat. Personally, I prefer mine from the butcher. I think Granny's butcher has a special stock of very old sheep out in his backyard that he kills when he knows we're coming for dinner. I just hoped Ivan would do his best with the roast potatoes and peas as he didn't eat meat if he could possibly avoid it.

'Ah … I think Poppet might need to go for a little walk outside in the fresh air,' Ivan said, pressing himself into the furthest corner of the car.

'It's just hiccups.' Dad lovingly stroked her head, ignoring the slimy dribble coming out of the sides of her mouth.

'She's going to be sick, Dad.' I moved in Ivan's direction. 'Stop the car Mum, Poppet's going to chuck!'

Mum slammed on the brakes and pulled the car over the side of the road.

'Steady on, Lyn.' Dad smiled sweetly at her. 'Don't overreact.'

Mum pulled on the hand brake and leant across Dad, shoving open the door. 'Quick! Get her out of the car!'

Dad struggled out the door as Poppet's sides began heaving. He put her down on the ground but didn't get out of the way fast enough as she vomited, catching his shoes and the sleeve of his jacket.

'Damn,' Dad said, looking at his clothes. 'Damn!'

'Don't let him back in the car, Mum,' I pleaded. 'Make him take his clothes off.'

'I'm not taking my clothes off in the middle of nowhere.' Dad looked about him wildly. 'There are some tissues in the back. Pass them to me, will you, Claire?'

'Put your shoes and coat in the boot,' I begged, handing over the box.

We finally persuaded the two of them to clean themselves up properly before they got back into the car. I won't go into unnecessary detail about what the rest of the drive was like. It should be enough for me to point out that tissues have never been proof against the stink of dog's vomit. Now all we had to look forward to was my grandmother's delightful dinner!

Chapter 6

'**H**e was so sweet,' Melissa explained at school the next day.

'But you went over there to kill him.'

'I know, but that was before I found out that the Metalica business was just a joke. He was going to tell me but I stormed out of the house before he got the chance. So anyway, when I got back he explained that he hadn't managed to get anything ready in time but that he'd worked out something really special.'

'Pretty strange sort of joke,' I grumbled. 'What's so funny about buying you something you're going to hate? Besides, it's a waste of money.'

'No, he's giving them to his brother. His brother loves Metalica. He just gave them to me to see what I'd say. He's a practical joker. You just don't know that side of him.'

'So, has he given you your real present yet?'

'I know what it is, but I haven't had it yet.' She nodded. 'As a matter of fact I owe Ivan some thanks. He put the idea into Warren's head in the first place. After I'd stormed out of Warren's place he was sitting around wondering what on earth to get me for my real present when Ivan dropped by. It's good they're getting on so well, isn't it?'

'Surprising,' I said. 'I don't think they're really each other's type though. It probably won't last.'

'Well, they seem to be doing pretty well considering. Anyway, they raved for a while and then Ivan suggested to Warren that he should get me something really unusual — something special.'

'Such as?' I stared deeply into to my sandwich, sensing what was coming.

'Well, you know how I used to hate sport?'

'Yeah.' I gave a mental groan.

'It's funny, but since I've been going out with Warren that's all changed. I really like playing sport now and I just love watching it. I don't know,' she shrugged, 'it's strange the way the more you give it a go, the more you get into it. I can't imagine how Ivan guessed, though, because I don't think I've talked to him about it since he's been back. But Ivan's always been sensitive, he must've picked up that my attitude had changed. So anyway, he suggested to Warren that he get us tickets for the races. And get this,' she paused for effect, 'Warren's getting us tickets for the Adelaide Grand Prix.'

I stared at her for a moment. 'But, Melissa, you hate motor racing, remember?'

'I *used* to hate it but after I had that argument with Warren everything changed. We've been watching it together on TV and I'm really into it now.'

'How can Warren afford the tickets anyway? People our age don't have that sort of money.'

'He works on the weekend at his mum's shop, don't forget. And I'm going to help pay for the flight over. I won't feel comfortable going otherwise.'

'And where are *you* going to get the money from?'

'I've got some left from the job I had over Christmas — simple.' She spread her hands and smiled.

'I don't know, Melissa.' I shook my head. 'I can't keep up with you. What does your mum say about it? Is she happy to let you go?'

Melissa let out her breath and made a face. 'I'm not absolutely certain what she thinks.'

'Meaning?'

'I haven't exactly asked her.'

'No wonder you're not sure what she thinks. May I suggest that she's not going to like it.'

'Don't be so sure,' Melissa said, stubbornly. 'I'm seventeen, remember. She knows that letting Warren and I go away together isn't going to be more than we can handle.'

'Since when has your mother been this picture of modern, liberal thought?'

'Mum's not old-fashioned about guys and sex.'

'Oh yeah? Well, let's just wait and see. When are you going to ask her if you can go?'

'I'll probably ask her tonight,' she said, as though it was no big deal.

'Well, you ring me up and tell me what she says. And this time don't forget me like you did the other day. By the way, thanks a lot for that.' I gave her a filthy look.

'Warren and I just got carried away, that's all.'

'Well there's no way you and your mum are going to get carried away, so ring me and tell me what she says.'

Of course I was right. You didn't need psychic powers to work out that Melissa's mother wouldn't be wild about the idea, especially since the Grand Prix was on just before the end of the school year. In fact, once Melissa's mum found out what was cooking, she rang Warren's parents and they all got together for a major gossip session and decided it wouldn't be good for either Warren or Melissa to take off for a weekend of wild sex and passion. Like I said, you didn't need to be an Einstein to work out what was going to happen. But poor Melissa, she rang me up in tears. I can undersand it, I'd be upset too if Ivan and I had something really special planned and our parents went and ruined it. It wasn't that I was going soft on Warren, but Melissa had looked so excited when she'd told me what they were planning. I tried out the idea on my parents just to be sure, but they thought Melissa's mum was right. They said it'd be different if a group of kids were going over together, but that at our age we were really too young to be heading off on our own. I'll tell you what though, it didn't seem like they were worried so much about the possibility that we'd have sex, it was more that they thought we shouldn't be doing stuff that was more for older couples like jetting around and having a good time. Personally, I couldn't see the subtle difference, but Dad kept rambling on about 'the intensity of the relationship'. Apparently, you could do it, but you couldn't do it in a hotel in Adelaide — that was adults for you. The most I could get out of them was that they'd say it was okay if we'd left school, but since we were still in our final year we had to be content with hanging out in groups instead of in pairs! I gave Melissa my parent's considered opinion, but the poor thing couldn't manage more than a groan of agony. After that we let the subject drop for about a week — it was just too painful to talk about.

Over that week I did some thinking and it seemed to me that I owed Melissa. I'd done nothing but plot against her boyfriend for the last four months, and I had to admit that plotting and scheming did tend to put a wall up between you and the person whose life you were trying to sort out. And when it really came down to it I guess I'd started to think that maybe I'd been a bit hasty in thinking Melissa didn't know how to take care of herself. I'll tell you what got me thinking. You know my brother, the one that lives with his girlfriend? Yeah, well he doesn't — not any more. You had to have known them before to realise how amazing it was that they'd split. They started going out together when they were both in Year 10 at school. I think big, passionate love affairs that last all the way through school are the absolute pits — strictly for dags only — but they seemed happy together and I didn't mind her, so I didn't give my brother too much of a hard time about it. Anyway, the minute they left school they got engaged — can you believe it? I think getting married is pretty suss in the first place, but getting down to it the moment you step out the school gates for the last time? No way! Of course my parents freaked right out and tried to ban everything that moved. My brother wasn't allowed to have his girlfriend over to stay. He wasn't allowed to ring her up. He wasn't allowed to talk about her. He wasn't allowed to mope around the house thinking of her. Well, after about three days of Mum's and Dad's treatment, he left home and moved in with her. In the end my parents resorted to bribery. They went over to my brother's for dinner and said that if he and his girlfriend put off getting married for three years, they'd help them buy their first home. Smart move. I think Melissa's mum had a hand in that tricky little suggestion because she and Mum spent hours talking about the most cunningly, evil ways you could get your children to do what you wanted.

So my brother and his girlfriend chose money over true love, and agreed to put off their wedding plans and everything went back to normal for about two years. In fact, until the night we went to Granny's with Ivan. Come to think of it, she was looking sheepish that night and my brother wasn't exactly in the best of moods, but you don't really notice these things, especially when it's someone like your boring older brother. Anyway, we got back to town and about half an hour later there was a knock on the door and in walks big brother to tell us that his girlfriend's left him to go and live in Rome with this Italian archaeologist. I couldn't believe it. She was this quiet, mousy little thing and all she'd ever seemed to want was to marry big brother, have lots of children, and look after the house.

I'll tell you what I think happened, though. I think Mum and Dad's plan worked even better than they could've imagined. Probably she got too big a taste of looking after a slob and decided there was more fun to be had in life. Good on her, I say. So I figured that if there was hope for her, there had to be hope for a superior being like Melissa.

The only trouble was Melissa didn't seem to recover from her mum's blow about not going to Adelaide. It was enough to make you depressed yourself, seeing the way she moped around school. She hadn't lost it completely, she still studied and mucked around and everything, that wasn't the problem. It was more that she'd stopped being her normal bossy self. We didn't really talk about it much, but I think her mum did a job on her — the old 'don't speak about him or think about him' trick. They never seemed to learn. But it wasn't until the following weekend that Melissa and I 'accidentally' discovered the depth of the adult conspiracy against the happy couple.

'Trouble is, she's still sulking,' Melissa's mum said. 'She won't even talk to me.'

'Honestly, Molly,' Mum answered her, 'you've got to ignore that. She's just trying it on.'

'Trying it on!' Melissa dug her fingers into my arm as we hid in the hallway. 'She's got a nerve.'

'Shssh!' I hissed. 'The door isn't that thick.'

I crouched down lower and found some room underneath Melissa. If I didn't mind the desperate cramp in my legs I could get one eyeball to the crack in the door and catch a glimpse of Mum and Melissa's mum hot at it over the kitchen table.

'I can put up with the silent treatment,' Melissa's mum continued, 'that's not the problem. Don't forget I've got twenty-seven years on her, but because she's my little girl I can't help worrying about her, Lyn.'

My mum snorted at the thought. 'Don't waste your time. She's as tough as old goats' knees.'

Melissa stiffened beside me. 'Don't pay any attention,' I insisted.

'I know she's strong. That's one of the things

I'm most proud of,' Melissa's mum agreed, 'but … Well, I guess I'm worried that she's depressed. If she were just being a nasty little pig about this business I wouldn't bat an eyelid, but she's not herself.'

'She's punishing you, Molly. And it's working.' Mum nodded her head, wisely.

'If her father were around things would be so much easier. At least then we'd be able to share the worry.' Melissa's mum sighed and took a gulp of coffee.

'Don't kid yourself.' Mum's eyes narrowed. 'Hollis was hopeless with Melissa. You're better off without him.'

'But at least there'd be someone else to share these things with.'

'Absence makes the heart grow fonder, my dear,' Mum said knowingly.

'I'd let her go if I thought she was old enough.'

'Are they sleeping together?' Mum asked.

'Who knows with a girl like Melissa. I mean, we probably would've been at her age, but we were different, weren't we? I mean we didn't have AIDS to worry about or this puritan trend that seems to be going on.'

'There's always something to worry about though, when you're that age.' Mum moved out of my line of vision and I heard her put the kettle back on the stove. 'Another one, Molly?'

'Yes thanks. Of course I bought her a whole lot of condoms just in case. I don't think you can expect kids to go and buy them for themselves, do you? It's pretty embarrassing.'

'In our day it was, but maybe it's different now.'

'Even then, I think I did the wrong thing,' Melissa's mum continued. 'I gave her the box and all she did was groan and look at me as though I was the dog's dinner.'

'No, you did the right thing,' Mum reassured her.

'What about you? What have you done about Claire?'

I nudged Melissa and nearly knocked her off her feet.

'Watch it,' she whispered, edging back into place.

'Well you know Claire.' Mum rolled her eyes. 'Pig-headed, know-it-all that she is. I started talking to her about different sorts of contraceptives and she announced that if or when she and Ivan decided to sleep together they certainly wouldn't be looking for my assistance.'

'She doesn't know her luck.' Melissa's mum sniffed in disgust. 'Remember what it was like for us?'

'Do I ever,' Mum agreed.

'They *are* better off now but let's not kid ourselves,' Melissa's mum tapped the side of her nose, 'fundamentally nothing's changed. Sure "nice girls in their late teens, who are going out with nice boys can do it", but you can't tell me things are easy for a girl who has sex with guys she's not in a relationship with.'

'You're right,' Mum agreed. 'The world's still a hard place for women. Hard enough without their parents making things even worse for them. Maybe you should've let Warren and Melissa go — enjoy themselves while they can.'

'You were the one who told me to follow my instincts,' Melissa's mum complained.

'The rotten cow,' Melissa whispered in my ear. 'To think it was all your mum's fault ...'

'Shut up,' I told her, putting my ear to the crack to catch what they were saying.

'... and then it wouldn't be so bad.'

'But that's not on the cards, is it?'

'What on earth are they talking about now?' I grumbled, pressing my ear closer.

'Well, we could do something about that,' Mum said.

'What? Organise it for them?' Melissa's mum sounded amused.

'It would be a lot of money, but maybe it's

worth it to see them happy. After all, they've got enough on their plates as it is. And once they leave school, they're going to find out that life's not much of a party despite the freedom of adulthood.'

'It's a bad time of year though.'

'Yes and no.' Mum looked thoughtful. 'It might do them some good to have a few days off before they have to start convincing the rest of the world they know what they're talking about. Those last few days are never much use for studying.'

'What about Gordon?' Melissa's mum asked.

'He'd probably say it was all right.' Mum sounded uncertain.

'Should one of us go with them?'

It was too much for Melissa. She grabbed my arm and started shaking it out of its socket to get my attention. 'Did you hear that?'

'I'm trying to.' I did my best to keep my ear to the door.

'Is that you, Claire?' Mum called out.

Melissa and I scuttled down the hall and hid inside the cupboard under the stairs just in time. I heard the kitchen door open and someone take a few steps into the hallway.

'There's no one here,' she called back into the kitchen. 'The little rats. I hope they weren't listening.'

'I wouldn't put it past them,' Melissa's mum said. 'Why don't we go over to my place for a while? We can go to the market on the way — I've got some stuff I need to pick up.'

'Good idea.' Mum's keys jangled as she dropped them into her bag. 'Let's go in your car, Molly, and then you can drop me home later.'

Melissa and I held our breath, praying Mum wouldn't decide to get her coat, but our luck held. The front door slammed and we were left crouched like a pair of freaks in the dust and dirt of the cupboard.

'Let's get out of here!' Melissa groaned, pushing open the door and tumbling out into the light.

'What do you think it means?' I asked her after we'd settled ourselves comfortably in the recently vacated kitchen chairs.

'It means they're planning to send all of us on a holiday.'

'Yeah, but who's all of us? Obviously Warren and you, and it sounds like I'm included too, but did they mean Ivan?'

'Why else the long dicussion about our sex lives. Nosy old cows.' Melissa scowled.

'I knew Mum couldn't wait to be let in on all of my secrets, but I didn't realise she and your mum compared notes. Remind me never to tell your mother anything ever again.'

'Me too.'

'So what do we do now?' I asked.

'We can't do a thing.' Melissa dropped her chin into her hands. 'We can't say anything, we can't even hint around the subject. As far as they're concerned we don't know anything about it, remember?'

'We'll just have to wait. How revolting,' I complained. 'For God's sake don't forget you're depressed — everything hinges on that.'

'So you'd go, would you?' Melissa asked. 'If they decided to go through with this, I mean.'

'Sure!'

'But you hate motor racing,' she pointed out.

'What's motor racing got to do with it?' I grinned. 'Who'd turn down a free holiday with you and Ivan to Adelaide?

'And Warren.'

I nodded. 'Yeah. And Warren.'

'You really don't like him, do you?'

I shook my head.

'Why not?' she asked. 'What makes him so awful that you have to constantly try to put me off him?'

'He's not smart enough for you, for a start. You're so clever,' I looked into her clear grey eyes, 'and he's got nothing up top. I don't know what you two find to talk about.'

'That's what I find so relaxing about him — we don't have to talk.'

'Going out with someone half your mental age is relaxing?'

'Yeah.' Melissa shrugged. 'I know you don't understand because you think that I should be head over heels in love with the person I'm with, but I don't look at it that way. I don't want to be in love with anyone but I can't see why that means I should have to miss out on all the good bits of having a boyfriend. Look at it from my point of view. Warren's really into me, he's got his own interests so he's not taking up too much of my time, and physically we're a really great match.'

'So you *are* sleeping with him.'

She nodded.

'You didn't tell me,' I complained, giving her a dirty look.

'Why would I tell you when you detested the sight of him? You weren't likely to adore the idea, were you?'

'I suppose not,' I agreed. Then I started to grin. 'So where do you do it?'

'None of your business.' Melissa put on her most superior face and looked down her nose at me.

'Come on, give me a break,' I complained. 'I

want to know.'

'His place or mine, it depends on whose parents are home.'

'I'm shocked.'

'You shouldn't be. Heaps of people do it, you know. What about you and Ivan?' she asked.

I shook my head. 'No, we don't.'

'Really?' She looked surprised. 'I was sure you would.'

'I just don't feel like it. The funny thing is we're sort of the opposite of you two.'

'How do you mean?' She looked puzzled.

'I really like Ivan. I really, really like him. Maybe I even love him ...'

'So?'

'It just doesn't feel right — physically I mean.'

'Wow!' Her eyes opened wide. 'I thought you and Ivan were really into each other.'

'We are, but all the same — hey, you won't tell Warren this, will you?' I shuddered at the thought.

'Are you kidding?' Melissa looked offended. 'That's not the sort of thing we talk about.'

'So you do talk. What do you say to each other?'

'Don't change the subject,' Melissa said sternly. 'You were about to tell me how you're really into Ivan and how you're not really into Ivan.'

'Sounds weird, doesn't it?' I made a face. 'I guess I can't explain it. I like cuddling up to him. I like kissing him. I like fooling around and acting as though I'd love to do it with him, but the truth is, I'd rather not. I don't know why.'

'Well don't then,' Melissa said, simply.

'I'm not going to.'

'So will it be all right in Adelaide? You won't feel like you have to or anything?'

'I know how to look after myself,' I laughed. 'Seriously, Melissa, can you imagine Ivan being able to get me to do something I didn't want to do?'

She looked at me for a minute. 'No,' she shook her head. 'You're probably the most stubborn, pig-headed creature I've ever met.'

'You sound just like my mother,' I told her.

Chapter 7

It was funny the way things changed after that day with Melissa. For a start I realised that although I'd been thinking of us as incredibly close friends, there were parts of her I didn't know anything about. You couldn't exactly say we'd drifted apart over the last couple of years because we'd kept on doing everything together like we always had, it was more that it'd been a while since we'd had a 'deep and meaningful'. Come to think of it, the last time Melissa and I talked about anything really personal was around the time her dad left her mum. That was strange for me too because my parents basically got on all right and when they didn't it was no big deal — not like Melissa's parents. Melissa's dad was a real pig. He used to do things to make Melissa think that the only reason his life was so off was that she was in it. It's strange the way someone as smart and nice as Melissa's mum could waste her time hanging around with someone like Hollis.

Melissa and I used to talk about how things were at her house all the time. Then, when her dad left, she used to talk to me even more because her mum was carrying on about how much she loved Melissa's dad and couldn't live without him. As you can imagine she didn't have any spare time left to see how Melissa was doing. At first Melissa was really pleased that her dad had gone, even though her mum thought it was a natural disaster, but then when he didn't even bother ringing her up on her birthday, and he never did anything about visiting her, it started to get her down. Not all that surprising really when you consider how fathers are supposed to behave. I complained about my dad liking Poppet better than me, but that's just his weird personality. He'd never forget something like my birthday, and in his own way he was into whatever I was doing at school. He even used to come down and watch me play netball — and that was genuine dedication, considering the fact he didn't have any idea what the rules were.

Anyway, you don't exactly go around talking

about heavy emotional stuff all the time — not even with people you really, really like, the way Melissa and I like each other. But talking to Melissa had made things better and I was glad we'd done it. It wasn't so much that we'd talked about Warren, it was more that now I understood what she was on about a bit more, Warren didn't matter so much. I guess seeing the way her parents had carried on had made her realise that being in love with someone can be a health hazard. Mind you, there was no risk I was actually going to start *liking* Warren just because Melissa and I finally understood one another. Let's face it, some things are simply impossible.

The next week and a half were the worst Melissa and I had ever had to live through. We told the guys what was going on — or what we *hoped* was going on. Naturally, Warren was rapt, but Ivan was a bit funny about the idea. As soon as things start looking up there's always someone who goes and spoils everything.

We'd arranged to meet the guys down at the rink and Melissa and I sprung it on them without any warning. Warren's eyes lit up and he grabbed Melissa and started trying to throw her up into the air. Since Melissa's a little too large for even a strong guy like Warren to go throwing around, he didn't get very far, but you could tell he was really excited. What with all the acrobatics going on beside me I didn't look at Ivan, then I noticed how quiet he was being. He left about ten minutes later. He said he'd forgotten that he'd promised to help his mother clean out the garden shed. Pretty weird if you asked me — especially since I later sneaked a quick look in the shed and found it absolutely undisturbed by any sort of spring fever.

I tried to corner him once or twice after that, but all he'd say was that he couldn't wait, that it was a terrific idea. Well you could've fooled me. It was like someone telling you they love your cooking while they sit there in front of you stirring their food around their plate without taking a bite.

Chapter 8

'So, Claire,' Dad looked at me over his bowl of Cornflakes, 'how are your studies going?'

'Fine,' I shrugged. 'You can never do enough, I suppose. At least, you don't know whether you're doing enough until you've finished.'

'But you've done well so far?'

'Yeah. You know that as well as I do.' I looked at him.

Dad scratched vaguely at his leg and then took up his spoon again and began to eat. He and Mum had usually left the house by the time I actually made it downstairs to eat my breakfast, but this morning Mum was loitering around and Dad seemed to have developed a bizarre craving for packaged cereal. I wondered what day it was and did a quick mental calculation. No, it wasn't their anniversary, it wasn't either of their birthdays, and it certainly wasn't mine. I had a feeling it could've been Granny's but they'd hardly be hanging around acting suspiciously if that was all it was. I looked over at Dad as he poured still more cereal into his bowl.

'What's going on?'

'Nothing.' He almost jumped out of his seat.

'Yeah, well I have to be going.' I stood up and picked up my plate and cup. 'I'll see you later.'

'Just a sec. I'll give you a lift as soon as Lyn's ready to go.'

'I don't need a lift,' I pointed out, 'my school's only two streets away, remember? I don't know what's going on with you this morning, Dad. Are you sick or something?'

'No, no.' He gave me a look of pure innocence. 'Just decided not to rush for once in my life.'

'Great.' I grabbed my bag. 'See you tonight then.'

'Ah, here's your mother now.' He got up from the table. 'We can all go together.'

'What's wrong with him this morning?' I asked Mum, as she sailed in the door, a briefcase under one arm and a pile of clothes for the drycleaners under the other.

'Wrong? There's nothing wrong,' she said, 'it's

just we wanted to tell you together and I've got a meeting this evening so we couldn't do it tonight.'

'Tell me what?' My heart started to flutter just a little. Maybe they really were going to let us go.

'Molly, your father and I, and Ivan and Warren's parents have decided that in view of the fact that it's only a matter of weeks until you finish school, you should be more than capable of going away together for the weekend. None of us liked the idea of Melissa and Warren going off on their own, so we decided to pool our resources and pay for the four of you as a special pre-exam treat.'

'I can't believe it.' I stood there grinning like an idiot. 'That's fantastic, Mum.'

'I must say I'm slightly surprised that this comes as such a shock to you.' Mum looked at me sceptically. 'Molly and I had our suspicions that you and Melissa knew what was in the air. Certain scratchings around the kitchen door several days ago ...'

'I don't know what you're talking about.' I gave her a wink.' Seriously though, we never thought it'd actually happen. I mean, we wanted it to and it was nice to imagine it happening, but we didn't think it would. And you're letting us go on our own?'

'You'd like one of us to come with you, would you?' Dad grinned.

'No need,' I told him, grinning back. 'No need at all.'

'Aren't you going to say "Thank you"?' Dad held out his cheek for a kiss.

I kissed them both and then raced them out the door and into the car. This was something that needed to be discussed in detail, but not with my parents. School's agony to sit through when you have stuff you're dying to talk about. I had to sit there for three hours trying to concentrate on what was going on and let me tell you, it wasn't easy. I could tell by the look on their faces that Melissa and Warren knew our parents were letting us loose, but I couldn't seem to catch Ivan's eye. Every time I looked over he was taking notes, or looking out the window — even leaning down to fix up his shoe laces. Typical Ivan, cool to the last. Probably he was bursting with the news, but didn't want anyone at school to notice. Ivan's always had a very laid back manner in public.

The first time I saw Ivan I thought he was a bit of a snob because he didn't seem to have anything to say and yet he looked as though he was letting everything tick over in his head while he sat back and decided what was what.

I'm not saying he was a snob, because I'm the first person to write off guys who sit back and judge everyone, but he did act like he was trying to perfect an image. He did seem like a border line case. So I kept clear for the first few weeks just to make sure he wasn't into looking down on everyone else from a great height.

Still, there was something about him that I liked — even back then when I didn't know anything about him. I'm not saying you can tell in some magical way what a person's going to be like just by looking at them, because that's just not true, but I do think you can know that you like parts of a person. Sometimes it doesn't mean anything. Sometimes it's just that they remind you of someone you like, or they do something that makes you laugh, but when you get to know them better you realise it doesn't go any deeper than that. But sometimes they really are showing a part of themselves.

With Ivan, it was his funny looking face that first made me think he mightn't be a bad sort of guy to get to know. It was like someone had put a hand on each side of his face and very, very gently moved one hand up and the other one down. His features didn't quite match. One eye was a little bit higher and a lighter shade of brown than the other, and his mouth and chin titled up on one side. You didn't see it the first time you looked at him. When you first saw him you just thought he was a good-looking guy with something quirky about his face. Then when you looked closer you realised what was so strange — that everything was out of alignment. It was even funnier when he smiled. When he smiled one side of his face swooped down and the other lifted right up. All the same, as nice as his face was, I wouldn't have been interested if he'd turned out to have a cold heart. I hate people like that.

When the lunch bell rang I headed outside to catch the first bit of spring sunshine we'd had for the year. There were wooden benches parked right up against the red brick wall of the school hall and if the sun was strong enough it was as though the wall was centrally heated. I leant my back against it to test it out. For a minute I felt nothing, but then the faintest bit of heat struggled through my shirt and jumper. It wasn't much, but at least it was something. I pulled out a sandwich, settled back comfortably, and waited for the others to appear. You can buy lunch at school and lots of kids do but my parents are convinced I'll become a diabetic if I eat canteen food. I keep telling them it isn't that bad and they keep making me these lunches that feature wholemeal bread and ridiculous amounts of vegetable matter. Today my sandwich was cream cheese, diced celery, carrot and salami — pretty nice actually. The only ones I really couldn't stand were the ones that had cold, wet bean sprouts dripping out the sides.

Melissa and Warren appeared about five minutes later. Melissa had a pie and a sausage roll — which was typical — and Warren had four, giant salad rolls. Warren eats excessive amounts of food because he thinks that's what all real men in training do. He's into building up muscle and bulk or something. I didn't pay much attention the last time he told me all about it.

'So,' he beamed at me, 'looks like me and Ivan have really struck it lucky.'

'Warren, please,' I groaned and put down my sandwich, 'get a grip on yourself. Yes, we are going away together. Yes, I'm going out with Ivan and you're going out with Melissa, but such events call for some decorum. If you're going to start behaving like some freak out of one of those American guys-can-never-get-enough teen movies then I'm going to ring your parents and tell them we're not going.'

'She's right.' Melissa made a face at him. 'Don't be a pain or we'll go without you.'

'Boy, a guy can't say anything around here

without getting into trouble.' Warren rolled his eyes. 'So what if I'm excited? It's only natural.'

'Where's Ivan?' Melissa looked around the yard, trying to spot him.

'I don't know.' I picked up my orange and started the revolting job of peeling it. 'I haven't had a chance to speak to him since my parents broke the news this morning. Was he in the canteen?'

'I saw him talking to a couple of people in the corner, near the big window,' Warren said. 'I waved as I went out the door,' he explained, his mouth stuffed with food. 'I presumed he'd follow me out.'

'Must've been held up,' I said, looking around the yard for about the third time. 'He's usually the first one out here.'

'It'll be a really nice end for his visit.' Melissa settled back and titled her face up to catch a bit of warm sun on her skin. 'He's not leaving till after the exams, is he?'

'I wish he was staying on for the holidays too,' I confessed. 'I've got used to having him around again.'

'I'd hate going out with someone I hardly ever saw,' Warren said.

'I dunno.' I smiled. 'It's got its advantages. You don't fight, you don't get bored with each other, you've always got heaps to talk about when you see each other, and best of all you don't have to worry about how to juggle your time between friends, boyfriend and study. No,' I shook my head, 'I don't think I'd have a boyfriend at the moment if I wasn't going out with Ivan. They're usually too much trouble.'

'Says who?' Warren started to puff out his chest.

'Says everyone who's got any brains at all.' I didn't bother looking at him, just closed my eyes and followed Melissa's example.

'You two aren't going to start arguing again, are you?' She sounded bored.

'No,' I said, 'just pointing out the brute facts to Mr Meathead here.'

'Okay, give me an example,' Warren said, starting to get excited.

'Melissa flopping around on the oval, dressed in the most ludicrous costume I've ever laid eyes on.'

'Oh no we don't!' Melissa sat up and opened her eyes. 'Not this again. I've had enough. Let's go inside, my bum's getting numb with cold.'

I thought I'd be able to catch up with Ivan after the final bell rang, but he was sitting near the door and disappeared before I had a chance to get hold of him. We had to try out for the athletics team right after school so instead of going straight over to his house, I spent the afternoon in my spikes running around the oval. I hate getting changed into my sports clothes when the weather's still freezing, but I knew I'd regret it later if I took the easy way out. Actually, Melissa was the one groaning the loudest in the changing room about the barbaric conditions the school imposed on us. She's got the sort of skin that starts going blue about the end of February and doesn't recover until late December. She's basically built for warmer climates — something her parents obviously didn't predict when they moved down from Sydney.

Despite Melissa's claim that she'd turned over a new leaf about playing sport, she stuck to her old favourites — archery, javelin, and shot put. I suppose I shouldn't say that, it's just that I don't really think of those sort of activities as sports. I know you have to be fit and strong and everything, but it's not the same thing as running — which is what I'm best at. Melissa likes it though. She hardly practices at all and then when sports day rolls around she starts throwing objects here and there and everywhere, and cleans up all the prizes. Now I wouldn't mind being able to do that but unfortunately I have to take my training more seriously. I don't do anything much in winter but by the end of August I usually start running after school.

We were out on the oval until it was dark. Melissa and Warren finished a bit before me but waited so I'd have some company on the way home. I knew Mum was going to be out at a meeting, but when I opened the gate the house looked down on me without a single light in any of the windows. I waved the others on their merry way and went inside to investigate what parental stuff up had led to my abandonment. Dad had left a miserable apology on the kitchen table suggesting I heat up yesterday's leftovers or grab some money out of the drawer and buy myself a pizza. About once or twice a week both of my parents ended up having to work late but usually they'd tell me in advance that I had to cook for myself, or Dad would fix one of his slow-cooking stews so it'd be ready to be taken out of the oven by the time I got home from school. I opened the fridge and peered inside. There was a brown glass bowl on the second shelf, nursing some suss looking spaghetti — the leftovers. No way! I pulled open the two bottom drawers to see what else I could find. The left one was completely empty and the one on the right contained five shrivelled mushrooms, two tomatoes, half a cucumber, and a very solid block

114

of cheese. Nothing doing.

When the phone rang I ran to answer it as though I hadn't talked to a living being for the last fifteen years. It turned out that it was only my brother, ringing to see if Mum was home. Since he didn't bother asking how I was I didn't waste much time on him. No wonder his girlfriend left him, I thought as we hung up. I reminded myself to get her address so I could write and offer her my congratulations. Come to think of it, having a contact living in Rome wasn't such a bad thing ... I almost went and found a pen and paper on the spot, but my stomach reminded me that there were more important matters to attend to — like food. Obviously I was going to have to go out and get myself a pizza so I might as well take it over to Ivan's place and eat it with him. No need to ring, Ivan's house was like a second home to me, but I did decide to take a shower and clean off some of the sweat I'd worked up.

The pizza shop was around the corner from Ivan's place so I was able to front up at his door with little wisps of steam rising out of the hole in the middle of the box. I'd ordered half hot salami and half vegetarian because of Ivan's phobia about meat. He'd eat it if he had to but basically the idea of chomping on dead animals didn't do much for him. Of course I agreed with him in principle, but sometimes I just felt I needed all the nourishment I could get.

As soon as Ivan opened the door I thrust the pizza into his arms and dashed inside.

'Boy, it's cold out there,' I said. 'I hope you haven't eaten already. Doesn't matter if you have though because I can eat it all myself. I just thought it'd be more fun to share it with you. Hey,' I looked around at him as he followed me into the kitchen, 'where were you today? You took off after class like a man on a mission.'

'I just wanted to get home.' He pulled a plate out of the cupboard for me.

'Aren't you having any?'

He shook his head. 'Mum and I ate early. She's got a new job.'

'Oh yeah, doing what?'

'Nothing much.' He put on the kettle and picked two cups out of the dish rack.

'Well, you're really the life of the party tonight.'

'Give it a break, will you?' he grumbled. 'I'm just tired.'

'Yeah me too,' I said. 'I tried out today.'

Ivan opened the coffee jar and spooned out the grains. He stood there stirring the dry mixture, around and around.

'Aren't you going to ask how I did?'

'How did you do?'

116

'Fine. I got into the team.'

'You always do.'

'That doesn't mean I don't have to try,' I reminded him.

'Eat your pizza,' he pointed at the cardboard box sitting in the middle of the table, 'it's horrible when it gets cold.'

'You sure you don't want any?'

'No you have it,' he insisted.

'Did your mum tell you the good news?' I asked.

'About the weekend of debauchery?' He sat down opposite me. 'Yeah. Pretty amazing, eh?' he said flatly.

'Don't sound so thrilled.'

'No, I am,' he tried to sound reassuring. 'I've just had a lot on my mind.'

'Like what?'

'Nothing I need to talk about,' he cut me off.

'Okay, I get the message,' I said. 'How's your dad?'

'He's fine.'

'So you'll be leaving as soon as the exams are over?' The prospect of Ivan's departure depressed me. 'I have to admit I've gotten used to having you around.'

Ivan stood up abruptly. 'Well, you'll have to get used to not having me around, won't you?'

'Take it easy.' I made a face. 'I don't know what's biting you tonight, but there's no need to take it out on me.'

'I'm not,' he stared at me, 'I'm just trying to face up to the truth. I'm not going to be here in about a month's time and I probably won't be back for ages. School's going to finish, I'll have to get a job or something, and I don't know when I'll be back. I don't even know if I'm going to pass the year.'

'You make it sound like you're never coming back.'

'I mightn't be.' He shrugged. 'Even if I do, you probably won't be here anyway.'

'That's true,' I admitted. 'I could be in Victoria or South Australia. I've applied.'

He gave me a look. 'Well there you go.'

'Even if it's true, even if we're not going to be seeing much of each other, that doesn't mean we should sit around being miserable *now*. After all, we've never seen much of each other and we've still had a really good time.'

'That was different,' Ivan pointed out. 'At least we knew when we'd be together. There was something certain about it.'

'There's nothing certain about anything.'

'Bull.'

'Well there isn't.' I picked up another piece of pizza and slapped in on to my plate. 'Anyway, what am I supposed to do about all of this? It's just the way things are.'

'Nothing. You're not supposed to do anything. I'm just pointing out that us going out together is pretty futile.'

'Maybe for you.' I swallowed a wad of dough to take my mind off the pricking feeling behind my eyes.

'If we were going to live together or something that'd be different, but our relationship's always been a bit of a joke.'

'Really?' I looked over at his angry, red face and hated him. 'Obviously it's been different for you than it has been for me then. I guess we've both been dreaming. Mine was a dream about two very good friends who were really into each other, yours seems to have been a different story altogether. It just goes to show how wrong you can be about what's really going on. I'll be seeing you.'

I picked up my bag and walked out of the room. Ivan didn't follow me. He just sat there. I could feel him behind me like a giant cloud of gloom. I'd never seen him like that before. My chest hurt from holding everything in and it was a relief to step out into the fresh air. I closed the front door behind me and headed for home.

Some people get into the drama of life. They

like pulling things apart and analysing every detail of their relationships, but I wasn't like that. I hated talking things over and over. I'd much rather forget about the bad stuff and get on with things. So when I saw Ivan the next day at school I just acted like nothing had happened. He'd probably had a really bad day the day before, and everything had looked extra bleak and sad to him. I didn't want to be the one to remind him about it. Probably if I reminded him about it he'd start feeling down again — and that was the last thing either of us wanted. All the same, I didn't spend much time with him. It was all very well him being upset about the future but he didn't have any right to take it out on me the way he had. No, he could come and be civil if he wanted to, but I wasn't going to throw myself all over him. If he wanted to forget about it and be his normal self again, then I'd do the same, but let him be the one to decide how things were going to be. As far as I was concerned, I could do without him. Sure, I'd miss him. Most of all I'd miss being friends with him, but he wasn't the only friend I had.

Melissa wasn't so cool about the whole thing though. She'd rung me the night before and squeezed it all out of me. I wasn't going to tell her, but she caught me at a vulnerable moment —

just after I'd arrived home and found that Mum and Dad were still out. So I spilled the beans, and because it'd just happened I was all over the place — one minute hating Ivan and the next dripping tears all over the phone. Then I had to spend the last ten minutes of the conversation making Melissa swear she'd instantly forget every word I'd said and that she'd rather die than let on to anyone — especially Warren — that anything unusual was going on between me and Ivan. She promised, but the next day at school she kept shooting me these looks of love and sympathy so I knew I was going to have to be more normal than my normal self if I was going to have any chance of dealing with the combined effects of Ivan and Melissa. As they say, 'With friends like these . . .'

Melissa stuck to me like glue. She followed me into the toilets, trailed around after me at lunch time, and kept suggesting I come over to her house after school. I even caught her throwing looks of hatred at Ivan as though he'd almost murdered her nearest and dearest friend. It was all too much. But she was so insistent that in the end I gave in and agree to spend the afternoon at her place. The most Ivan got was a smile and a wave as she pulled me out the gate at three-thirty. She had hold of one side of my schoolbag and was using her not inconsiderable weight to keep me moving in the right direction. I guess that's what happens when you have the school shot put champion as your best friend.

Chapter 9

Mum stood in front of the door blocking my exit. 'You know perfectly well that we're going to Granny's this weekend.' She ran her fingers through her hair while Dad removed some delicacies from the fridge and put them carefully into a cardboard box. 'I'm not going to fight about it, Claire,' she said. 'You're coming and that's that. It's a perfect opportunity for you to get on with your study. You can make up for the time you'll lose when you're in Adelaide.'

'Can't I stay here and work?'

'No,' Dad said, lifting the box up into his arms. 'But you'll be pleased to hear that Poppet's not coming this trip.'

'I don't believe it.' I raised an eyebrow

questioningly at Mum.

'I bumped into Ivan at the shops and he said he'd look after her for us. Mum's worried about her neighbour's sheep. Apparently there have been a few killed. Not that Poppet could've done it ...'

'But we don't want her shot by mistake,' Dad cut in.

'That puts a different complexion on things. Can Melissa come too?'

'No.' Dad edged past us, out the kitchen door. 'This is going to be a family weekend.'

'I hate family weekends,' I groaned. 'Of all the mean and nasty things to scheme up ...'

'Just you watch your step, young woman,' Mum warned.

It's easy to get carried away giving your parents a hard time. It's almost like they go around asking for it. But the truth was, I actually liked it at my grandmother's. What I couldn't get into was the way Mum and Dad organised things without asking if it suited me. They always assumed I was going to be doing what *they* decided I was going to be doing. In lots of ways my parents were cool. They didn't insist on knowing where I was and what I was up to every minute of the day, but they still didn't treat me like I was a real person. They treated me as though I was their property — like I was a big dog without any fleas. If they kept it up after the endof this year I wouldn't be hanging around for long.

Mind you, I probably wouldn't be around for long anyway, not if things went the way I'd planned. I intended to be off to college and a whole new life of excitement in a few months time. But I wasn't going to think about that, not after Ivan's little performance the other night. It was amazing the way guys could spoil something you'd been looking forward to for so long. But I wasn't going to think about that either. Guys were out, the future was out, the weekend in Adelaide was probably out too — maybe it was just as well we were going to Granny's for the weekend, otherwise I'd drive myself crazy trying to keep my mind off forbidden subjects.

I went up to my room and packed a few things. Riding boots, gum boots — it was still pretty wet — jeans, a couple of jumpers, socks and a few T-shirts. The main items were my textbooks, but I snuck in two novels to relieve the pressure. I could hear Mum and Dad laughing hysterically as they stacked stuff into the car. I went over to the window and looked down. Dad was sitting on his bum on the driveway, almost wetting his pants while Mum pointed at him and fell back against the car, weak with laughter. It looked like Dad had fallen over which just went to show the sort of intellectual level I was going to have to deal with all weekend. I lifted up my case and carried it outside. I only hoped a bit of civilised behaviour wasn't going to be too much to expect from the pair of them.

With Poppet leaping all over me, we drove over to Ivan's house. I hadn't seen much of him at school and although nothing bad had happened since our fight, nothing good had happened either. In fact, we'd hardly seen each other. Dad handed me a five kilogram bag of dog food and I struggled out of the car. It was no easy matter to get Poppet in the gate and up the path to Ivan's front door without falling flat on my face. I opened the flywire door and leant up against it to maintain my balance. With one hand gripping the leash for dear life and the dog food in the other, I used my shoulder on the doorbell. Ivan opened the door and I fell inside.

'I've got Poppet.' I handed over her food before I dropped it.

'Yeah, I can sort of tell.' He smiled and closed the door. 'Let her go, she can run around the house for a while.'

'Sorry about this.' I waved my hand after the disappearing dog.

'That's okay.' Ivan put her food down on the carpet. 'I volunteered, remember? Do you want to come in?'

'Mum and Dad are waiting in the car.'

'Oh.'

'So I guess I better get going,' I said, brightly.

He took a step closer. 'I'm sorry about the other night.'

'It doesn't matter.'

'But it does, doesn't it?'

'A bit,' I admitted.

'I love you.' He put his arms around me and pulled me to him so I could feel all of his body leaning against mine. He was shaking a bit.

'That's nice,' I said, nervously. 'A bit of a change of tune though, isn't it? I thought our relationship was futile, according to you.'

'Honestly, Claire,' he looked at me hopefully, 'I really didn't know what I was doing. I was so miserable about everything coming to an end... You're the only person that matters to me,' he said, quickly.

'Take it easy.' I laughed and pushed him away. 'I dunno about you guys. Hot one minute, cold the next.'

'Seriously.' He put his fingers to my lips to stop me from going on. 'I really love you.'

'Yeah, well I love you too, Ivan. But listen, I

always have loved you — you're my friend.'

He sighed. 'And I suppose that's just the way it is. You love me like a friend.'

'There's nothing wrong with that. That's the best sort of love I've got. It means more than being "in love" — whatever that is.'

Ivan buried his face in my shoulder and then rubbed his cheek against mine. Finally we found each other's lips and it was a relief to feel close again despite his un-Ivan like confessions of undying passion. We stood in the hall, kissing and holding each other until the car horn sounded.

'Oh God,' I groaned. 'I forgot about them. You sure do pick your moments. There we were the other night,' I swept my hands around the hallway, 'with hours to ourselves, and you decide to stage a major crisis in our relationship.'

'Stay here with me for the weekend.' Ivan leant forward and gently kissed the soft patch of skin beneath my ear. 'Mum wouldn't mind.' He ran his finger down my spine persuasively.

'Oh really? Well, unfortunately, my parents *would* mind. I've got to go, Ivan, but I'll be back. Sunday around seven-thirty... I'll give you a ring then.'

Chapter 10

The next few weeks we were all flat out. Ivan was trying to make up for lost time before the final end of school year crunch, so he hardly spoke to anyone. I was in training and pacing myself for the exams at the same time. Melissa was studying hard and Warren was doing whatever it was that Warren did. I didn't ask what he was up to because we'd settled into some sort of harmony where we all met at lunch time, didn't hassle each other, avoided talking about anything to do with school or relationships, and then all disappeared in different directions after the bell went. I guess a wild social life is out of the question when you've got a whole lot of other things on your mind. It was a relief when our school sports day came and there was a break in the study-eat-sleep routine. Best of all, I knew that once sports day was over, I'd only have the exams left to concentrate on and then I'd finally be free.

Sports day was great, actually. Not only was the weather fantastic, we all picked up a few prizes — all except Ivan who isn't into physical activity. I came first in four events and third in another two, Melissa won every event she entered without actually moving more than about two metres in any direction, and Warren starred in a meaty sort of fashion.

Part of the reason why sports day was always so good was that the whole school, even the kids who weren't in any of the teams, had to come along and join in. Then, that night, there was the sports day dance. The kids who weren't competing were responsible for setting up the school hall and decorating it with house colours, and usually we had a school band playing. There'd been a couple of years where our musicians had been so hopeless that we'd opted for tapes instead, but a live band was always better. This year we had an all-girl band with two sax players, a drummer, and a guitarist — everyone reckoned they were the best band the school had ever produced.

The good thing about being in Year 12 was

that we didn't have to do anything except enjoy ourselves. The other years were responsible for making all the arrangements, getting the food together, and cleaning up afterwards. As soon as I'd finished competing I went and sat next to Ivan on the grass. He had his back against the fence so I rested my head in his lap and stared up into the deep, wide blue of the sky. We must've stayed like that for about two hours. Whenever it was time to turn around and watch some event Ivan would tap me on the forehead and I'd turn around, but basically we got into the day rather than the competitive side of things. Melissa joined us about halfway through and Warren arrived just in time to watch the winning house captain accept the sports day cup from our headmistress.

We were at a loose end after that with four hours to kill before the dance was due to start. After we'd showered and changed we decided to walk down to the local shopping centre to fill in time. Not that we did anything really interesting once we got there, but it's incredible how much fun it was just hanging out after weeks of being locked up with our books. Give me a couple of cheap thrills and I'm yours for life. We played the pinnies and the video games, went and listened to a few discs at the music store, and rode on those rides they have for the little kids. The security guard put an end to that bit of fun pretty quickly — we got a lecture on how at our age we should have more respect for other people's property and didn't we know that the rides weren't designed for giants. That sort of thing always happens to people our age.

'Come on, let's get out of here.' Warren heaved himself off the tiny red and white airplane he'd been sitting on.

'Pity,' I said, crawling out of the Flintstone's car, 'I was enjoying that.'

'I don't know,' Ivan shook his head, 'you pay your money like any other juvenile and just because your parents have brought you up on a diet of Vegemite and cheese sandwiches, they discriminate against you. I can't help it if I'm an early developer.'

'Go on, get out of here,' the guard said. 'You ought to know better. What would your parents say?'

We left him hovering around the rides and grumbling about vandalism, and walked down to the sliding glass doors of the centre. There was a pet shop just before the entrance to the car park and I made everyone stop while I went in search of puppies. I mightn't like fat, hairy golden retrievers who vomited in cars, but I'd kill for a cuddly little ball like the ones sitting in the pet shop window. They always made me so sad though. Mum and Dad used to make my brother and I go in and out the back way when we did the shopping on Saturday mornings because they couldn't bear to listen to us going on about how much we wanted a puppy. That was when we were younger, of course — in the early days, before Poppet arrived.

If you were in Year 12 you weren't supposed to go anywhere near the hall until eight o'clock, so we had to circle the school four times waiting for our watches to hit the hour. It was a ritual. The younger kids were meant to surprise us with how amazing everything looked. And it was pretty amazing too. The minute it turned eight Sophie's and Christie's saxophones started to blow and the air turned electric. The two of them jammed for about ten minutes while everyone filed in and then Emma and Helen joined in and we knew the party had begun.

Ivan and I were on our feet the whole time. We'd dance a couple of songs and then we'd look at each other as though we couldn't take another step without a break, step off the floor for a rest, and the band would start playing something we couldn't bear to miss out on so we'd find ourselves back on the floor again. It went on that way all night. Not that we only danced with each other. Melissa and I bopped around together for a while and I also danced with this guy I did all of my experiments with in Chemistry. Warren tried waving me over to dance with him a couple of times, but being familiar with his dancing style I kept clear. Also, he had this awful habit of coming too close to you. Maybe that was all right with Melissa, but I wasn't going to subject myself to it — not even for the sake of friendship.

Melissa and Warren left early, but Ivan and I hung on until the very end — until we had to be kicked out by the headmistress. That's the trouble with school socials, they end before you get a chance to really get things moving. We talked about going on to a club or something but apart from the minor problem of being under age, neither of us had enough money for the taxi fares so we ended up going back to Ivan's house. His mother was out at work whereas my parents were probably sitting around the living-room just waiting for the chance to corner us, so the decision wasn't a difficult one.

'Put on a tape or something,' I threw myself into an armchair, 'I can't handle this silence.'

'What do you want to hear?'

'Anything, anything,' I waved my hand in his direction, 'just so long as it's loud and good.'

'You're easy to please.' Ivan laughed, turning up the volume until I could feel the sound pounding on the walls of the house.

'Your neighbours are going to love this,' I shouted.

'To hell with them!' he shouted back.

The music was so good and we still had enough party mood left in us, to get me up out of the chair I'd fallen into to, and the two of us out into the middle of the floor for fifteen minutes or so. I finally slowed down when my feet began to hurt and the neighbours started to bang on the dividing wall.

'I'll put something soft on,' crooned Ivan, working the stereo.

'Time for a little romance?' I matched his tone.

'Has anyone ever told you what a gorgeous woman you are?'

'Constantly.' I went and arranged myself on the couch.

'Your eyes...' He began to glide towards me.

'Go on.'

'Ah... Your lips...'

'This is so original.'

'Your nose...'

'Get on with it, will you?'

'To the couch!' He dashed the last few steps towards me and landed, less than softly, on top of me.

'Thanks a lot,' I complained, struggling to breathe. 'By the way, isn't this couch a little too small?'

'Do you want to come into my room?' he asked, no longer joking.

I nodded and we walked down the hall holding hands.

Chapter 11

It was cold in Ivan's room but nothing could touch me. I was warm from dancing and warm with the feel of the night. I looked over at Ivan. His hair was damp from all the bopping around, and it curled in ringlets about his ears. His shirt hung out and his skin felt hot to touch in the chilled air of the back of the house. I wrapped my arms around his neck and we let ourselves down on to the bed.

'Shall we get in?' he asked.

'I think so, don't you?'

'Seems like a good idea,' he agreed.

We pulled off our shoes and jeans and slipped under the covers. It felt strange to have another warm body in a narrow single bed instead of finding myself alone in my own. I held Ivan to me and felt the touch of our toes, knees, and chests.

'Just imagine,' I stroked his face, 'we can do this all night in Adelaide. I won't have to worry about Mum and Dad waiting up and you won't have to think about what your mum's going to say if we're still in here by the time she gets home.'

He stiffened, slightly. 'Let's not talk about Adelaide. Let's talk about something else.'

'Why?'

'It's nothing.' He tried a nonchalant shrug. 'I just don't feel like it, that's all.'

'Come on,' I complained. 'You can't get away with that. Explain!'

'Actually, I'm thinking of backing out of the whole thing. I just don't want to go. It's not my sort of scene.'

'Ivan,' I pulled his face towards mine and looked at him closely, 'what's going on? This is Claire you've talking to, remember? We don't have to sleep together if that's what you're worried about.'

'It's not that,' he laughed shortly. 'That's the least of my worries.'

'Well then, what is it?' I pressed.

'I can't talk about it.'

'Can't or won't?'

'Can't, Claire. There are some things you can't talk about even if you want to.' His voice rose a little. 'Look, this involves someone else and it wouldn't be fair to them if I told you.'

'I don't believe it,' I started to laugh. 'What are you talking about? Don't tell me you've got a second girlfriend hidden away somewhere and you've promised her you won't go. That you'll tell me it's all over between us as soon as school's finished —'

'Don't be stupid,' he snapped.

'Well, *tell* me then!'

'I can't.' He gritted his teeth and stared up at the ceiling.

'Right.' I ripped back the covers and sat up. 'I'm going. If you think it's okay to lie here in bed with me when you can't even share one little problem with me, well you're wrong. That's not the way things work.' I stood up and pulled on my jeans. 'Let me know if you change your mind — but don't wait too long because I'm not going to be around if this is the way you're going to carry on. Honestly, Ivan, I'd have thought I'd be the first person you'd feel you could confide in. Why else do you go out with someone unless they mean something special to you? Obviously, it's not the same for you though ...'

'Okay!' He sat bolt upright and glared at me. 'If you really want to know, Mum can't afford it. It's all right for you lot, your parents have all got money, but Mum… Well, she's not working night shift for the fun of it. In case you hadn't noticed, until this job came along she was out of work for four months — and Dad's been sick.'

'Why didn't she say something?'

'Oh yeah?' He looked at me bitterly. 'Such as what? Being broke isn't exaxtly the sort of thing most people brag about.'

'So she said you couldn't go.' I sat back down on the bed.

'No,' Ivan shook his head, 'she said I could go, but I know she can't afford it. I don't want her to waste her money on a stupid visit to the Adelaide Grand Prix. I don't even like car races. Why should she work herself into the ground so I can keep up with the rich kids.'

'I'm not a rich kid.'

'Yes you are. You just don't know it. You think because you don't have a swimming pool and a tennis court and all that, that you haven't got much money. You wouldn't even know what being short of money felt like.'

'There's no need to attack me,' I complained. 'Okay, so we were all a bit blind and thoughtless, but that doesn't make us all that different from you. We might not be short, but we're not millionaires.'

'But you've never had to worry at night about

whether you're going to be able to keep your home or not, have you?'

'I'm sorry, Ivan.' I lay back down and put my arms around him. 'I didn't realise. I'm not surprised you don't want to go. I guess… I guess I'll just have to go on my own — what a bummer. I mean I understand and everything, but I was really looking forward to being with you.'

'Don't talk about it,' he groaned. 'Think about what it's been like for me. I knew weeks ago that I'd have to find a way to get out of this trip and all the time all I wanted to do was get on that plane and be with you.'

'How can life be like this?'

'That's just the way things are.'

'But it's so unfair.'

'Come on,' he pulled me to him, 'it's not that bad. You're such a drama queen. Bad is when you can't pay the bills or you don't have enough to eat, and here we are whinging about not being able to go on a luxury holiday together.'

'Yeah,' I sighed, 'I guess you're right.'

Chapter 12

It looked like things had really taken a turn for the permanent worse. Ivan wasn't going to be able to come, we only had a couple more weeks of school left before he'd be leaving for his dad's place, and I couldn't talk about the Adelaide problem with anyone because Ivan had made me promise not to tell.

All Melissa and Warren could do was rub salt into the wound. Not that they meant to of course, they were just full of the great times we were all going to have once we got on that plane. Melissa even went ahead and booked the rooms and the seats in the airplane for us. I stalled her on paying for anything because I knew there was no reason why we couldn't do that at the last minute, but I couldn't think of a way to tell her Ivan wasn't coming without breaking my promise about keeping quiet.

Obviously I'd have to tell them that it was going to be just the three of us at the last possible minute. Imagine it though — the three of us — me, Melissa and Warren. All those months of planning and scheming to get rid of the creature, and I ended up going on holiday with him! *I* was going to be doing *him* a favour. I had to be out of my mind. Either that, or my luck was at an all time low.

Ivan and I spent hours and hours sitting around his kitchen table after his mother had gone to work, trying to work out ways to solve the problem. My big contribution was buying two lottery tickets but neither of us were all that surprised when I didn't win. Ivan went on a selling spree to try to raise enough money. He sold the electric guitar he never used, some computer games, his leather jacket, and a few other bits and pieces, but he still didn't have enough. What really got me down was that I wouldn't have minded forgetting the whole deal and staying home, but if I backed out Melissa and Warren wouldn't be allowed to go. And that'd been the whole point of the exercise in the first place.

The other reason why I spent so much time

at Ivan's house was that my parents were full of the holiday and how much fun it was going to be, and when *they* weren't going on about it, in would waltz Melissa demanding that we work out what clothes we were going to wear and exactly what the sleeping arrangements were going to be. I could've told her in an instant — on my own in one room and her and Warren in another — but a promise is a promise. To say that studying wasn't easy was putting it mildly. In the end, I took all my books over to Ivan's and we got into it together. In a way that was the best solution because there was no way we could talk round and round in circles about the holiday while our heads were deep in our books. Killing two birds with one stone, you might say.

Of course the inevitable happened. I'd avoided Melissa pretty successfully for a couple of weeks, but a few days before we were due to leave she landed on my doorstep with a look of grim determination in her eyes.

'Oh,' I looked around wildly, 'I was just going out...'

'Were you?' She smiled at me and pushed her way past me and into the house. 'Let's go upstairs. I need to talk to you.'

'I can't Melissa — honestly. I've promised Ivan

'Last time you'd promised Ivan's mother that you'd help her with her tax return. That was your mistake, you know.' She turned around on the stairs and wagged her finger at me. 'People do their tax in July or August, Claire, not late October.'

'But that's why she needed help. She had to get it in before she got into trouble. You get fined if you don't.'

'And you're such a great accountant. Tell me all about it.'

I followed her into my room. 'I guess I just have a knack with numbers.'

'Bull. You've been avoiding me.'

'I have not,' I insisted.

'Don't lie, Claire. I know you so well. Something's up and you're going to tell me what it is or I'm not leaving this room ever again.'

So it tumbled out. I'd done my best, I really had, but there came a point where being loyal to Ivan definitely got in the way of being a true friend to Melissa. And I'd known Melissa for longer, so I guess you could say that she won out. She heaped it on me for not telling her sooner. My excuses about promises to Ivan were totally irrelevant as far as she was concerned.

'So how much money has he got from selling all those things?'

'Three hundred and fifty dollars.'

'That's enough,' she said, looking more cheerful.

'Enough for the airfare, but there's accommodation, meals, and other expenses.' I shook my head. 'It's not enough.'

'Well,' Melissa said slowly, 'how much money have you got?'

'A couple of hundred, but I was going to use some of it as spending money.'

'How much could you spare?'

'I don't know.' I thought about it. 'I guess about a hundred and fifty.'

'Me too.'

'But, Melissa, it's one thing for me to help Ivan, but you're not going out with him.'

'Maybe not,' she shrugged, 'but I've been friends with him for just as long as you have, and I want him to come just as much as you do. Why shouldn't I chip in?'

'He won't take it.'

'How do you know?'

'He wouldn't want to borrow money he couldn't pay back. You know what Ivan's like. Besides, even if he did, it still mightn't be enough.'

'He will take it because we're going to give it to him, not lend it to him. We'll pay for the flight right now and then he'll be throwing away our money if he doesn't come. Besides, his mum can chuck in a bit. If she was going to pay anyway I'm sure she'd want to contribute something.

'He won't like us going and doing it without asking him first,' I pointed out.

'No,' Melissa agreed, 'but then again, if that's the only way to get him to come, then we've got no choice, have we? Let's do it.'

'Now?'

'Right now.'

Chapter 13

Two days later, the four of us piled on to an aeroplane. I'd never been on a plane before and neither had Warren. It must've been the first time we'd actually had something in common. I scoffed all the food, read all the magazines, used the toilets, and drank all the free soft drinks they offered me. If you're paying all that money, I figure you owe it to yourself to get the most out of it. Ivan and Melissa cracked a few weak jokes about the return flight not being able to lift off the ground if I kept it up. I didn't take any notice though, I wasn't going to miss out on one minute of the experience.

We caught a taxi from the airport to our hotel in the centre of town. It was an old five-storey building with bow windows and balconies and it had a roof that was all peaks and little red domes. They looked like witches hats — nothing like those great ugly modern buildings most cities are so full of. It must've originally been an apartment building or a convent or something because inside it was like living in your own flat. Each room had a kitchenette, a sitting-room, bathroom, bedroom and a balcony that you could step out on to.

Of course I was supposed to be sharing a room with Melissa, and Ivan and Warren were meant to be down the hall, but I don't think our parents took that seriously for a minute. Anyway, we weren't going to waste our holiday wondering whether they'd meant what they said. What they didn't know certainly wasn't going to hurt them.

We'd arrived around dinner time so once we'd taken a look at each other's rooms and half unpacked our cases, we went in search of food. The hotel didn't really have a restaurant, just a poky little coffee shop that none of us wanted to be seen dead in so we walked along the mall and then down towards the river in search of something better. Maybe it was unrealistic to think that life was going to be full of these sort of adventures once school had finished, but it felt good — no doubt about it, it really felt good to be out on our own. We found an Italian place that was so full of people all talking at once, that I didn't think we'd even get in the door. But when Melissa decides she's going to do something there's no stopping her. She pushed her way in through the door, elbowing about ten people to one side, and somehow caught the waiter's attention. I wouldn't say it was instant service, but we got a table and a whole lot of cheap and delicious food.

After we'd eaten we wandered back towards our hotel. It was late enough to go to bed, and I had to admit none of us minded the idea of turning in early, but somehow it didn't seem right that the night should end so quickly. The streets were crowded because of the race the next day and the shops were doing a roaring trade selling food and drinks to all the tourists so we walked back past the turn off to our hotel and on down Rundle Street. About ten minutes later we came across a little place with music and noise pouring out in all directions.

'Looks like this is it,' Warren said.

'Warren,' I took his arm, 'I've got to admit that for once in your life you're right.'

'In we go, guys,' Melissa said, taking Ivan's arm.

We danced and hung out raving until about one in the morning when they started closing down for the night. The streets weren't as crowded as we walked back to the hotel, but you could still feel a bustle in the air telling you that this was a special weekend. And it was a special weekend too. Special for all of us, but especially for Ivan and me because we'd come so close to missing out on being together. We took the lift up to the third floor and said goodnight to Melissa and Warren on the landing.

'What room is it again?' Ivan asked.

'Three thirteen,' I reminded him. 'Have you got the key.'

'Of course.'

'Let me open the door. I've always wanted to do this — open the door to my own hotel room.'

Ivan handed it over and we stepped into our apartment. It was completely dark, but we didn't turn the lights on. I walked over to the bay window and pulled back the curtains. The night light streamed inside. I turned around and found Ivan facing me.

I squeezed his hand. 'We finally made it.'

'Thanks to you and Melissa.' He put his arms around me. 'I haven't had a chance to thank you both yet...'

'Well let me tell you this,' I pinched his cheek, 'we're not going over to their room at this time of night.'

151

'No risk of that.' He smiled at me. 'Anyway, it was you I really wanted to thank. I wanted this so much, and somehow you did it.'

'Enough talk,' I said, putting my fingers to his lips. 'Let's go to bed.'

Titles to enjoy in the *Lovelines* series

Melinda Houston
Shy Girl £2.99

If you're pretty shy and you've lived in the middle of nowhere all your life, then moving to the city can rate high on the stress scale. Kate may be smart at school, but there's so much she doesn't know about — she's always tempted to crawl into her shell when things get rough. But local hero Pete Shardlow seems to like her anyway. Pete's so cool and confident that it takes Kate a while to realise she can help him as much as he helps her. All she knows at first is that meeting Pete has changed her life forever . . .

Phoebe Dalle
Opposites Attract £2.99

Sometimes Alison wonders how she and Richard ever got to be friends at all – the only thing they have in common is that they're both crazy about animals. Alison knows exactly what she's going to do with her life – she's wanted to be a vet for as long as she can remember – and her new after-school job with the local vet is a fantastic opportunity for her. But Richard just seems to drift through life in a daze, and Alison can't believe how slack he is about his future. She's looking for someone with a bit more ambition – maybe the vet's law student son, Blair, could be the one?

Kimberley Gregg
Something About Zac £2.99

There's only one thing that matters to Cathy Connolly. Swimming. It should be simple, but lately life seems to be getting more and more complicated. Cathy's dad pushes her so hard, nothing ever seems good enough for him. The school swimming teacher has a real grudge against her. And it looks like Fiona Evans, Cathy's arch rival, will stop at nothing to make her life miserable. The only bright spot on the horizon is swimming star David Hollis. It certainly looks as if David might be interested in her — but just how far will Fiona go to ruin Cathy's happiness?

Karen Miller
Winner Takes All £2.99

Marlee's had a tough time with all the problems at home, but things
are definitely looking up now that her dad has moved out. And then
there's Zac, Marlee's new boyfriend, adding some excitement to her
life. Zac has everything going for him – brains, looks, *and* money.
Marlee wishes things were so easy for her; she reckons Zac's got it
made. But slowly Marlee starts to realize that Zac's life isn't as perfect
as it seems . . .

All Pan books are available at your local bookshop or newsagent, or can be ordered direct from the publisher. Indicate the number of copies required and fill in the form below.

Send to: Pan C. S. Dept
             Macmillan Distribution Ltd
             Houndmills Basingstoke RG21 2XS
or phone: 0256 29242, quoting title, author and Credit Card number.

Please enclose a remittance* to the value of the cover price plus: £1.00 for the first book plus 50p per copy for each additional book ordered.

*Payment may be made in sterling by UK personal cheque, postal order, sterling draft or international money order, made payable to Pan Books Ltd.

Alternatively by Barclaycard/Access/Amex/Diners

Card No.

Expiry Date

_____

Signature:

Applicable only in the UK and BFPO addresses

While every effort is made to keep prices low, it is sometimes necessary to increase prices at short notice. Pan Books reserve the right to show on covers and charge new retail prices which may differ from those advertised in the text or elsewhere.

NAME AND ADDRESS IN BLOCK LETTERS PLEASE:

....

Name _____

Address_____

_____

_____

_____

6/92